BENJAMIN DRAGON
AWAKENING

BENJAMIN DRAGON
AWAKENING

Book 1 of The Chronicles of Benjamin Dragon

C. G. COOPER

ISBN: 1533245649
ISBN-13: 9781533245649

(http://www.BenjaminDragon.com)

To my amazing wife who never tires of my outlandish stories,
I love you, K, and couldn't do it without you!
To my entire family and amazing group of friends that have
supported me unconditionally. You guys are awesome.
To all you amazing kids, feed your talents, don't wish away
your youth and always make new friends.

CHAPTER 1

BULLIED

The boy shuffled slowly down the bright school hallway. Papers fluttered on the ground as he passed and the smell of the French fries from lunch lingered in the air. There was more trash around because of the flyers for the dance on Friday. Benjamin wouldn't be going. His father had said he should ask someone, but who would he ask. Benjamin didn't have any friends.

This was his second school for the academic year. Moving was part of Benjamin's family life. They'd moved again because of his mother's job. His father also traveled all the time to help companies fix whatever they were doing wrong. Sometimes he came home after what he called a "restructuring trip." Benjamin knew that meant he'd had to fire people from their jobs. His dad, usually loud and happy, was always quiet after those trips. He'd sit watching ESPN with a distant look in his eyes, not really watching. Benjamin made sure he got his dad extra beers on those nights.

The school bell rang. Doors opened with crashes along the hall and students rushed out, chatting excitedly with their classmates. Benjamin kept his eyes glued to the paper in his hands. It was a class schedule the school counselor had given him. Advanced English, Advanced Algebra, Advanced, Advanced, Advanced. It was his first day at the new school. He'd eaten his packed lunch by himself.

Benjamin was a smart kid…a really smart kid. He was only ten but his parents and the school system had agreed that he should skip two grades. There weren't many public schools that could give him what he needed in his age appropriate grade. Sometimes Benjamin wished he wasn't so smart. Nobody had asked him if he'd wanted to skip grades.

Walking through the throngs of locker-slamming kids, Benjamin peeked up every few quick steps. The last thing he needed was to bump into someone. He was almost a head shorter than most of the others. Embarrassing.

Thankfully, he made it out of the crowded school and onto the bus waiting area. He looked for bus 29, the one with Mrs. Wilkinson driving. She was nice. Old, but nice. Benjamin just hated how she talked to him like he was five. There was always a hint of pity in her eyes.

Bus 29 wasn't parked yet. That meant he'd have to wait. Benjamin pulled the cell phone his mom had given him out of his jean's pocket. No messages, no texts and no missed calls. Typical. All the boys and girls around him were texting and checking their Facebook accounts. Benjamin wasn't allowed to have a Facebook account yet. His mom said it would expose him to bad stuff. He had one anyway. His parents didn't know about it. He knew more about computers than they did.

Benjamin checked his Facebook account and breathed a sigh of relief. There was a message from Erica, one of his only friends from his old school.

how was your 1st day?

Benjamin typed a quick reply.

i survived

As he closed the app, Benjamin got bumped to the side by a group of three larger boys. The biggest one turned with a sneer.

"Watch where you're going, shrimpy," he said.

Benjamin didn't say anything. He knew it was better to just be invisible. This time, that tactic didn't work.

"I said, watch where you're going," the boy growled. His friends watched expectantly.

"I'm sorry," Benjamin offered quietly.

"What did you say?"

"I said I'm sorry."

"Sorry doesn't cut it around here, new kid. What's your name?"

"Benja…"

"Oh that's right!" the boy turned to his friends. "I heard Miss Lesindry talking about the new kid. He has some funny last name." Turning back to Benjamin. "Isn't that right, shrimpy?"

Benjamin closed his eyes for a second and took a deep breath. His hands shook.

"I asked you a question, shrimpy. What's your last name?"

More kids were crowding around the humiliating scene. Girls and boys pointed at Benjamin.

"Dragon," he whispered to his feet.

"Say it louder, shrimpy."

3

Benjamin looked up slowly. "My name is Benjamin Dragon."

The small group howled with laughter. Taunts flew at him from all directions.

"Look at the little dragon!"

"Breath fire, dragon!"

"Where are your scales, dragon?!"

Unseen by Benjamin, one of the other boys snuck up behind him and pulled Benjamin's pants down. He stood silently, eyes as big as saucers, a sheen of tears coating them. Benjamin finally got the nerve to bend down and pull his jeans back up.

Someone started a chant that quickly spread. "Dragon, dragon, why your pants saggin'? Dragon, dragon, why your pants saggin'?"

With eyes watering, Benjamin tried to push his way past the older students.

"Where do you think you're going, saggin' dragon?!" the ring leader yelled.

He grabbed Benjamin by the collar and threw him to the ground. The crowd yelled, "Fight, fight, fight…!"

No adults came to Benjamin's aid.

"Get up and fight me, saggy draggy."

Benjamin looked up in despair. He raised his palms and noticed that he'd skinned his hands on the concrete. Blood seeped out in tiny lines.

"Aw look at saggy draggy, he's got a boo boo. You get a boo boo, saggy?"

Benjamin got to his feet and wiped his hands on his jeans. His mom wouldn't be happy. She always liked him to be 'presentable.'

A single tear dripped from his right eye and fell onto the pavement.

"Look at saggy, guys. He's crying. Maybe we should call his mommy."

The laughter and jeers hit a new level of hysteria. Boys and girls fed off the charged energy. It felt like an electric current passing through the group.

Without warning the bully rushed Benjamin. The crowd hushed and time slowed. It seemed to take forever for the two to connect. Benjamin raised a hand, palm out, just like cops you see directing traffic. It couldn't stop the bully. Benjamin closed his eyes.

The collision never happened. Later students would tell the principal that the new kid had punched Nathan (the bully) in the chest. If anyone had looked closely, they would have noticed that the two boys never touched. Instead the bully was thrown back like a bullfighter getting slammed by a bull. He flew back into the crowd.

Benjamin examined his hand in shock as if expecting to find a gun held tight. There was only the scraped and bleeding heel.

The crowd hushed. Then the whispers started. Someone was trying to wake up the bully.

"What's going on here?" the adult voice came out of nowhere.

Children scattered, leaving the bully lying on the ground and Benjamin standing with mouth hanging open.

The teacher looked down at the boy on the ground then back up at Benjamin.

"What happened here?" the teacher asked with a scowl.

"I don't...I don't know..."

The teacher yelled for help and three other teachers materialized. Where had they been two minute before? Stupid teachers.

One of the teachers bent down to check the bully.

"He's breathing," she announced.

The first teacher pointed a finger at Benjamin. "You are coming with me to the Principal's office."

Benjamin's head dropped to his chest as he followed the man back into the school.

What a great way to start at a new school.

CHAPTER 2

QUESTIONING

They'd waited for Benjamin's parents to arrive. He'd had to sit outside like a criminal. The security guard had taken away his backpack and cell phone.

Now Benjamin sat across from the Principal, Mr. Kent, flanked by his two parents. They were both in their work clothes. Benjamin's father, who was smiling affably, wore an expensive pin striped suit that perfectly fit his athletic form. He'd loosened his tie.

Benjamin's mother sat with a frown in her grey skirt and blue blouse. Her suit jacket was folded on her lap. She'd been in a courtroom when the school called. She was a lawyer and the reason they moved so much. They had to move from big case to big case for something she called 'litigation'.

Benjamin's parents were both very attractive. The perfect power couple.

"As I was saying, Mr. Dragon.." said Mr. Kent.

"Please, call me Tim."

"Thank you, Tim. As I was saying, the young man your son assaulted is now lying in the hospital emergency room. It looks like he has multiple broken ribs. We cannot let this go unpunished."

Benjamin's mother spoke up. "How is it that this even happened, Mr. Kent? Surely you have staff that monitor the children so no one gets bullied. Especially the new students?" She arched an eyebrow. It was one of her signature courtroom moves.

Mr. Kent nodded. "We do, Mrs. Dragon, but it all happened so quickly and we can't have eyes everywhere. Like I mentioned earlier, the testimony we've gotten so far from the student witnesses..."

"Testimony? Were they under oath, Mr. Kent? Because I find it very hard to believe that my son started the fight or that he assaulted the other boy. Have you asked Benjamin what happened?"

Everyone looked at Benjamin.

"We, uh, haven't had a chance to..." started Mr. Kent.

"Okay then," said Tanya Dragon. She faced her son. "What happened, Benjamin?"

There was little compassion in her eyes. She was all business. It was a show for her to put on in front of the principal.

"I...I don't know," stammered Benjamin.

"Come on, Benjamin. Just tell the truth," his mother prodded.

Before he could answer, the Assistant Principal stuck his head in the door.

"We just took a look at the surveillance video, Mr. Kent."
"And?"

"It looks like the Pratt kid.."

"Nathan," said the Principal.

"Right, Nathan Pratt. It looks like he was the one who started the whole thing."

"What about how Mr. Pratt got hurt? Did my son punch him like the other kids say?" asked Timothy Dragon, a small hint of pride creeping into his voice as he glanced at his son and winked.

The Assistant Principal stepped all the way into the office and scratched his balding head. "Well, the angle of the camera didn't give us a clear picture. It looks like Nathan Pratt rushed your son and then went flying backwards."

Benjamin's mom looked triumphantly back at the Principal. "There you have it. Benjamin is not responsible. It sounds like he protected himself."

Sweat dotted Mr. Kent's blotchy forehead. He adjusted his necktie nervously.

"Yes that may be the case, but..."

"There is no BUT, Mr. Kent. Are you running a zoo around here? Do I need to get on the phone with the Commissioner? I'm sure he'd be excited to learn about the bullying that goes on under your roof," said Mrs. Dragon.

Mr. Kent looked at his Assistant Principal with beseeching eyes, then back to the fiery eyes of Mrs. Dragon.

"School policy states that any student engaged in fighting will be automatically suspended, Mrs. Dragon. My hands are tied," he almost pleaded.

Tanya Dragon shook her head slowly. Timothy Dragon looked on with a tight smile. He knew the drill. His wife could crush the toughest opponent in or out of the courtroom. It was one of the reasons he'd fallen in love with her.

"So let me get this right, Mr. Kent. If a student is attacked by another student, the student should just lay down and take it?"

Mr. Kent's mouth opened and closed like a goldfish. No words came out.

"What's the verdict, Mr. Kent?" asked Mrs. Dragon.

The principal grabbed the back of his neck and squeezed like it hurt. He tried to match Tanya Dragon's stare.

"As I said, it's not my decision.."

"You're the principal for God's sake! My son was assaulted and now you want to punish him. What's it gonna be, Mr. Kent?"

The principal's eyes looked like they wanted to pop out of his head.

"I suppose we can allow Benjamin to attend in-school suspension for one week."

"Not good enough, Mr. Kent."

"Mrs. Dragon, I'm sure you understand the spot you're putting me in. Nathan Pratt's parents are very well respected in this town and I have a set of rules to uphold."

"You let me worry about the Pratts, Mr. Kent. I want you to make this situation disappear or I'm going to the commissioner and the local newspaper. I'm sure other parents would like to hear about how you're allowing students to be assaulted."

The threat hung in the air like a throbbing fireball. Neither side wanted to touch it. Mr. Kent looked like he was about to have a heart attack.

"Very well. No suspension."

Tanya Dragon stood up quickly, followed by her husband. Benjamin remained in his seat, looking glum.

"Thank you for your time, Mr. Kent. Come on, Benjamin."

Benjamin stared up at his mother and sighed. Looking like he was carrying a hundred pounds on his shoulders, he stood up and followed his parents out of the principal's office.

CHAPTER 3

REPERCUSSIONS

No one said a word as the small family climbed into Mr. Dragon's BMW. Benjamin sat in the back staring at his knees.

His mom turned around in her seat. "Are you okay, Benji?"

Benjamin nodded, but kept his eyes downcast.

"Look at me, honey." The lawyer voice was gone. She was his mom again.

He looked up at his mother and he couldn't stop the tears. They ran freely in steady streams and cascaded down his cheeks and onto his mussed shirt.

"I'm sorry, mom. I didn't…"

"It's okay, honey," she said as she handed him a tissue.

"I'm proud of you, buddy," said his dad. "Your first fight. I remember my first fight. I was in third grade. The kid's name was…"

"Not now, Tim," Benjamin's mother said.

Mr. Dragon shrugged and refocused on the road ahead.

"Are you okay, Benji?" she asked. "Let me see your hands."

Benjamin sniffed and wiped his nose. "I'm fine, mom. And it's Benjamin, remember?"

Mrs. Dragon put her hands up in surrender. "Sorry, sorry, I forgot. But you know you'll always be my Benji, right?"

Benjamin nodded at his smiling mother. She didn't always understand him, but she tried in her own way. It wasn't easy being an only child to two parents like his. They were so successful and popular. Benjamin was almost the opposite. He wished he could be like them sometimes.

His mother patted him on the leg. "Where would you like to go eat to celebrate your first day at your new school?"

It was a ritual they had every time they moved. Since he could remember, his parents tried to lessen the sting of a new home by spoiling him a little bit. They thought they could somehow distract him of the fact that he'd have to figure out a new house, new school, new teachers and trying to find new friends.

"I'm not really that hungry, mom."

"Why don't we go home and get changed. I'm sure you'll feel better after a quick shower. I heard they've got one of those great wood fire pizza places you love."

⬤

By the time they got home it was decided that Benjamin's dad would go pick up the pizza and bring it back to the house. They were still unpacking, but they could sit on the couch and eat. Mr. Dragon always made sure the TV was the first thing installed when they moved to a new home.

After carefully rinsing his injured hands, Benjamin soaked in the hot shower. He let the soothing stream spill down his body. Losing all track of time, he closed his eyes, replaying the fight in his head.

A knock on the door shook him from his thoughts. It was his mom.

"Honey, dad's back with the pizza. Come get some before it gets cold."

"I'll be right down, mom."

With a reluctant look he shut off the shower and grabbed his towel.

Three minutes later he walked downstairs, pulled by the smell of fresh hot pizza. His favorite was pepperoni, mushrooms and basil with lots of cheese.

Coming into the living room he saw that his dad was watching some sports show on TV, cramming pizza into his mouth as he sat glued to the commentary. His mom was at their small dinner table leafing through work files as she picked at a mixed green salad. She never ate much. Benjamin didn't know how she did it. She looked up as he ambled in.

"You'd better get some before your father eats it all." She motioned toward the kitchen counter where an enormous pizza box sat with its lid cracked open. There was a picture of a fat Italian guy with a white hat tossing a pie into the air on the top.

"Smells good," said Benjamin.

"It is," said his dad through a mouthful of cheese and mushroom.

Benjamin grabbed a plate and loaded it up with two huge slices. They were so big that they flopped over the ends of the plate and drops of pepperoni grease dripped onto his hand. He attacked the pizza as he walked to sit down on the couch. His dad glanced over.

"Slow down there, champ. Don't want you to get a stomach ache," he chuckled.

Benjamin nodded and swallowed. "I didn't know how hungry I was."

"That's what happens after a fight, buddy. All that adrenaline goes away. Always happened to me after a big game. There wasn't a buffet on campus that could fill me up." Benjamin's dad had been an All-American quarterback in college.

"Guarantee you'll sleep like a baby tonight."

Benjamin looked tired. Dark circles threatened to drag his eyes down past his nose. He yawned before taking another bite of pizza.

His mom walked around the couch and sat down next to him. Benjamin's dad got the clue and clicked off the television.

"Honey, I wanted to talk to you about the fight today."

"Mom, I..."

"Don't worry, I'm not angry and neither is your father. We just wanted to find out exactly what happened."

The look of sincere concern on their faces wasn't normal. Benjamin knew his parents loved him, but they usually left him alone. He didn't blame them. He'd learned to take care of himself.

Tears came to his eyes as he recounted the tale.

"Are you sure you didn't hit the other boy?" asked his dad.

Benjamin shook his head.

"So how did he get thrown back, Ben?"

His dad always called him Ben and his mom called him Benji. It was one of those weird things that parents do. It's like they think they own a different part of you. Weird.

"I guess I must've just pushed him really hard," said Benjamin.

Everyone was silent for a moment as they digested the story and their dinner. Benjamin wiped his eyes and yawned again.

"Why don't you go get some sleep, honey," said his mom.

Benjamin didn't protest. After a kiss on the cheek from his mother and a pat on the shoulder from his dad, Benjamin made his way back up to his bedroom.

His head hit the pillow and immediately he fell into a deep slumber.

CHAPTER 4

FRIENDS

Benjamin was dressed and ready for school when he sauntered downstairs for breakfast.

"Good morning, sunshine," his mother called from the kitchen bar. The always-present mountain of paperwork rested next to her meal of grapefruit and non-fat cottage cheese.

"How do you eat that stuff, Mom?"

"What? The cottage cheese?"

He nodded.

She shrugged. "I guess it's an acquired taste."

Benjamin opened the fridge and looked inside. Someone had placed the leftover pizza into an oversized Ziploc bag. He opened it and grabbed a piece. His mom noticed.

"See, I don't know how you eat cold pizza for breakfast," she said.

"I guess it's an acquired taste, Mom."

She rolled her eyes and refocused on her work.

"Do you mind if I walk to school today?"

"Actually…I know you're not going to like this, but I think we should go to the hospital to check on that boy."

Benjamin's eyes went wide.

"What?"

"Look, honey. I know what I said in the Principal's office yesterday, but I've found that sometimes just going and saying you're sorry works wonders."

"I don't know, Mom…"

"Do you trust me?"

Benjamin nodded glumly. Could he really say no?

They both finished their breakfasts and headed to the garage. Benjamin slowly climbed into his mom's Lexus and buckled himself in.

———

Ten minutes later they arrived at the local hospital. Benjamin's mom asked for Nathan Pratt's room number from the white haired lady at the information desk.

"Room 402."

"Thank you."

Benjamin skulked behind his mom as they boarded the elevator.

When they reached Nathan's room, the bully was talking to two adults. It turned out it was his mom and dad.

Benjamin had expected a lot of screaming, all directed at him. None of that came. Mr. and Mrs. Pratt were really nice. They both apologized to both Benjamin and his mom then made a red-faced Nathan do the same.

"I'm so glad you both came," said Mrs. Pratt.

"We were just talking about calling you," said Mr. Pratt nervously. He was wearing soiled overalls with a logo on the front. Benjamin didn't recognize the company. "I just want to let you know that Nathan will be properly punished for what he did."

"I'm so glad to hear you say that, Mr. Pratt," said Mrs. Dragon. "What do you say we adults go out in the hall and let these two make-up?" She smiled sweetly to her son. He knew that look. It was the same look she'd given him before he had his first swim lesson. It was like she was saying, "You'll do it and you'll like it," with a smile, of course.

The Pratts agreed and left with Benjamin's mother.

The two enemies were alone. Neither knew what to say.

"So what are you in for?" Benjamin asked cautiously, thinking a joke might cut the tension.

Nathan grinned. "The usual. Labotomy."

The two boys laughed nervously.

"I'm sorry about hurting you," offered Benjamin.

"It was my fault, dude," he winced after saying 'dude.'

"What's wrong?" asked Benjamin.

Nathan grimaced and waved his hand. "No bigs. Just a couple busted ribs." He patted his chest gingerly.

"Doesn't it hurt?"

"It's not so bad with the drugs. I hope they give me some for home."

"Yeah. That would be sweet."

"Yeah. They make me a little funky in the head."

"I bet."

An awkward silence blanketed the room.

"When do you get to go home?"

"They said sometime today. I don't mind it so much, but I don't think my parents are happy about paying for it."

"Paying for what?"

"The hospital bill."

"Oh."

"Yeah. My dad'll probably make me work it off down at the car shop. That's what I had to do when I ran mom's car into a light post."

"You can drive?!"

Nathan shrugged. "Kinda. My grandpa taught me how to drive his truck out on the farm he used to work on."

"That's cool."

"Yeah."

"So how did you wreck your mom's car?"

"I took it out one night when my parents were working late. Tried to keep it on the down low by keeping the head-lights off. Made a turn too quick and BAM. Bye bye light post."

Benjamin laughed. "My parents would've killed me."

"I thought mine would too. Got grounded and had to fix it myself down at the shop."

"You know how to work on cars?"

Nathan nodded. "Started messin' around in the garage when I was a kid. You know anything about cars?"

"Nope."

"Too bad."

"Maybe you could teach me?" Benjamin suggested.

Nathan paused to think about the request. "As long as you promise to not chop your finger off."

"Okay."

Before they could finalize their plans, the three parents re-entered the room.

"Everything okay in here?" asked Mrs. Pratt.

The two boys nodded.

"Good because I've invited the Dragons over for dinner."

Benjamin and Nathan moaned and rolled their eyes. Why do parents always make you do things you don't want to do?

CHAPTER 5

DISTRACTED

The other kids stared at him all morning. Was he destined to be the school freak until graduation? Benjamin tried not to think about it and worked hard to focus on what the teacher was saying. He kept his eyes downcast taking detailed notes.

"So when General Washington got the news about advancing British forces…" droned Mrs. Dewberry. Benjamin probably knew more about history than she did.

Distracted, he doodled a picture of George Washington standing on top of Mrs. Dewberry's head. It was a good likeness. He wasn't happy with the way he'd drawn Mrs. Dewberry's dress. Turning his pencil over to use the eraser, it slipped out of his hand and fell to the floor. No one noticed.

Benjamin bent over to pick up the pencil. Before he could grab it, the pencil hopped up into his hand. Benjamin jumped in surprise, knocking his textbook to the floor in the process. The room went quiet as the students' gaze flew at him. His face flushed deep red.

"Is there a problem, Mr. Dragon?" Mrs. Dewberry asked, crinkling her nose impatiently.

"Uh, no Mrs. Dewberry…sorry."

"That's alright. Now please retrieve your textbook so that I might continue."

Benjamin hurried to comply. The blonde haired girl sitting next to him giggled and whispered to her friend. People were pointing.

"Eyes on me, students!" Mrs. Dewberry ordered, punctuated by a clap of her hands.

Benjamin relaxed. He inspected his pencil carefully. No strings. No magnets. How had it flown up into his waiting hand? First the thing with Nathan and now this? What was happening to Benjamin Dragon?

CHAPTER 6

THE PRATTS

The Dragons pulled up to the modest one-story brick home. There was a mailbox out front that had *Pratt* hand-painted in flowing yellow lettering.

"I guess this is the place," announced Mr. Dragon.

A tingling mist came down as they hurried to the covered front stoop. Mrs. Dragon rang the doorbell. Mrs. Pratt answered a moment later.

"Tanya and Tim, welcome!" she said with a smile. "How are you, Benjamin?"

"Fine thank you, Mrs. Pratt."

She let them in and called for the rest of family.

Benjamin looked around the living space. It was warm and inviting. The smell of baked bread mingled in the air. There were a lot of pictures on the walls and knick knacks on the shelves and side tables. Everything looked well used but tidy.

Mr. Pratt walked into the room and shook Mr. Dragon's hand. "Welcome to our home. Can I get you all anything?"

"I'd love a beer, thanks," said Mr. Dragon.

"And you, Tanya?" Mr. Pratt asked.

"A glass of water would be wonderful."

"You got it. Tim, you wanna come give me a hand?"

Mr. Dragon followed Mr. Pratt to the kitchen. They were already discussing something about restored cars.

"Nathan, come out and say hello, honey," Mrs. Pratt called out.

A moment later, Nathan shuffled out. He went to wave a greeting but winced in pain.

"Ow," he said.

"Still hurt?" Benjamin asked.

Nathan nodded.

"Nathan, why don't you show Benjamin around the house. Dinner's in ten minutes," said Mrs. Pratt.

"Okay, Mom."

The two boys headed toward the back of the house. They stepped into what could only be a boy's bedroom. Video game and music posters covered almost every wall. A wooden loft bed sat propped over a small desk. Benjamin examined the room.

"You like Deadmau5?" he asked, pointing to a poster with a Mickey Mouse looking head on it.

"Yeah. You?"

"Yeah."

Nathan took a seat on the edge of his bed. He eased himself down slowly, closing his eyes slightly.

"Whatcha been up to?" Benjamin asked, still looking around the small bedroom.

"Just watching TV."

There was an uncomfortable silence as both boys searched for something to say.

"How was school?" asked Nathan.

"Sucked. Everybody was looking at me like I was a weirdo."

"Sorry about that."

"It's okay. I'm used to it."

"You guys move a lot?"

"Uh huh. My mom's job."

"What does she do?"

"She's a lawyer."

"What about your dad?"

"He fixes companies."

"My Dad said he played football in college."

Benjamin nodded.

"That's pretty cool. You play football?"

"My dad wishes. You?"

"Sometimes."

"Why's that?"

Nathan looked embarrassed. "I got kicked off a couple teams when I was little. My dad knows all the coaches, but no one wants me on their team. He says it'll change when I can play for the high school team. I'm gonna try out next year."

"Can I ask you something?"

Nathan cocked his head to the side. "Yeah?"

"Have you always bullied other kids?" Benjamin asked quietly.

Again the uncomfortable pause. Finally Nathan answered.

"I guess."

"Why?"

The larger boy's shoulders shrugged.

Before they could continue their conversation, Mrs. Pratt called them to the dinner table.

◆

The rain had stopped by the time dinner they'd finished dinner. Nathan took Benjamin out to tree fort in the backyard.

The dads were in the garage looking at the old Bronco Mr. Pratt was restoring. The moms were drinking coffee in the kitchen.

"Wow!" exclaimed Benjamin. "Did you make that?"

A smile crept onto Nathan's face.

"Me and my dad did."

"That's awesome."

They climbed the eight foot wooden ladder and entered the covered structure. Nathan breathed heavily as he squeezed over the ledge. There was enough room for four or five other kids. Benjamin wished he had one in his yard.

"So what do you do out here?"

"I used to come up here with my dad. Now that I'm older I come up here to get away and read."

"What do you like to read?"

"Not what you'd think."

"Why?" asked Benjamin.

"I like stories about magic and knights. You know, fantasy and sci-fi stuff."

Nathan avoided Benjamin's gaze by picking at a piece of splintered wood on the wall.

"That's cool."

"You want to tell me how you stopped me from knocking you down?" Nathan asked, still avoiding Benjamin's look.

Benjamin's mouth opened. He didn't know what to say.

"I don't know."

Nathan's eyes flashed and then mellowed.

"Did you pull out some crazy karate stuff on me?"

"I don't think so. I've never taken karate."

"Brazilian jiu jitsu?"

"No."

Nathan scratched his head.

"All I remember is you putting your hand out and them I'm flying back. It felt like a truck hit me."

Benjamin shrugged.

"I don't know."

"Maybe you have magic powers."

The boys stared at each other and then burst out laughing.

"I wish!" Benjamin managed to blurt out between heaves and giggles.

CHAPTER 7

THE INCIDENT

The next couple weeks went better than Benjamin ever could have imagined. He and Nathan had become friends and spent most of their afternoons together. Sometimes they would work at Mr. Pratt's auto shop and other times they would hang out in Nathan's tree house.

To Benjamin's surprise, Nathan was pretty smart. He did a lot to hide that fact from the other kids at school. Benjamin asked Nathan about it once.

"It's easier to be the big dumb kid I guess," he'd said.

Nathan's 'friends' hadn't been too happy about Benjamin. They'd tried to press Nathan into not hanging out with the new kid, but Nathan instead stopped hanging out with his old friends.

They ate lunch together, taking over a small table in the corner of the lunch room. Slowly, and one by one, a couple of Nathan's friends mellowed and rejoined their leader.

There was Little Mikey, who was as short as Benjamin despite being two years older. He had more confidence than anyone Benjamin had ever met, except his own parents, of course. Sometimes he would walk down the school halls singing at the top of his lungs. Luckily, he was a good singer and the teachers didn't really mind. They thought it was funny.

Funny Paul came next. He was always telling jokes and making farting noises. Everybody thought he was hilarious.

Last came Aaron. He was almost as tall as Nathan, but pretty quiet. When you first met him it felt like he looked at you with mean eyes, but it turned out he was just shy. Nathan told Benjamin that Aaron was pretty smart too.

Together the five boys would walk the halls joking and laughing. Gone were the days of picking on other students. Nathan had squashed that. He'd told the other boys that he'd learned his lesson because Benjamin was so cool. That made Benjamin happy.

The older boys treated Benjamin kind of like a mascot, but at least no one was staring at him anymore.

There hadn't been any more 'incidents' as Benjamin liked to call them. He'd tried to make his pencil do the floating thing again whenever he was at home doing his school work. It never worked. Maybe he'd just imagined it.

One day Benjamin and Nathan decided to walk home instead of taking the bus. It was only a couple miles and luckily they lived in a safe town. There hadn't been a robbery in over ten years.

They were discussing the latest book they'd both checked out from the library. Something about dragons, knights and wizards. Neither of them was really paying attention as they crossed the street next to the grocery store.

A loud screech stopped their conversation. They both looked up. Just over a block away an old rust-lined car swerved its way into the intersection. It seemed like the driver couldn't keep control.

"I'll bet his brakes went out," said Nathan.

Following the path of the vehicle the boys saw a girl with brown hair approaching the intersection. She had white earphones on and was completely oblivious to the car.

Benjamin yelled for the girl to move. She didn't hear him. The boys starting running toward her.

The car barreled in and was now maybe a hundred feet from the unsuspecting walker. As the girl went to step off the sidewalk she glanced up slowly. Her eyes widened and she froze.

"Move!" screamed Nathan and Benjamin at the same time. They were too far away.

The car's path now determined, the girl finally crouched down. As if that would do anything.

Benjamin reached out his hand despite still being half a block away. That's when something amazing happened. Instead of continuing the remaining feet and slamming into the girl, the car lifted slightly and flew straight left. It came to a crashing halt as its side slammed into a building fifty feet away from where its path had changed.

Nathan stopped, but Benjamin kept running. He knelt down by the girl who was now lying on the ground sobbing.

"Are you okay?" he asked.

She just looked around unable to answer.

Nathan walked up not saying a word, his face a mix of shock and confusion.

"Can you go check on the driver?" Benjamin asked his friend.

Nathan nodded wordlessly. Then, as if he'd just woken from a dream, he shook his head and sprinted across the street. People were coming out of the shops lining the avenue. Some had cell phones to their ears as they peered out in concern.

Three police cruisers showed up two minutes later along with an ambulance. The driver of the car and the girl on the ground were quickly loaded into the waiting ambulance. As the only real witnesses to the event, aside from the injured driver, Nathan and Benjamin were taken to the local police station for questioning.

The police officer driving Benjamin and Nathan had instructed them to call their parents. Mr. Dragon was out of town on business. That left Benjamin with only the option of calling his mom while she was in court.

Mrs. Pratt and Mrs. Dragon showed up at the police station shortly after their boys arrived. Benjamin and Nathan had already been questioned on the way over.

"Are you okay?" Mrs. Dragon asked her son as she examined him from head to toe.

"I'm fine mom. We were just there when it happened."

"What did happen?"

Benjamin told his mother the story.

"It was a blessing the car swerved at the last second. That little girl could have been killed!"

Benjamin nodded sheepishly, but it was Nathan who interjected.

"The car didn't swerve."

Everyone looked at Nathan.

"What do you mean, sweetie?" Mrs. Pratt asked, concerned.

Benjamin shot Nathan a pleading look and shook his head ever so slightly.

"I…I'm not sure," stuttered Nathan.

"Well I'm just glad everyone is okay. What do you say I take you all for an early dinner? My treat," said Mrs. Dragon.

They all quickly agreed. Benjamin nudged Nathan on the way out the door, but Nathan ignored him. Benjamin's face drooped as they walked out to their mother's cars.

CHAPTER 8

ALONE AGAIN

A week passed and Benjamin kept getting the silent treatment from Nathan. His calls and emails went unanswered. Nathan wouldn't even talk to him at school. It was as if he didn't exist, again.

Benjamin was so confused. His ten-year-old mind tried to unravel the mystery. He'd thought they were becoming good friends, maybe even best friends. That was something Benjamin had never had. He longed for it.

The one bit of good news was that Emily Newsom, the girl who'd almost been run over by the car, started talking to Benjamin at school. They didn't eat lunch together or anything, but it was nice to have someone to say hi to or just wave at between classes.

Benjamin almost jumped when his cell phone rang. He hadn't gotten a call in almost a week. He'd been so engrossed in his homework that it took him a second to process the name on the screen: *Nathan Pratt*.

Benjamin quickly answered the phone. "Hello?"

"Hey," said Nathan.

"Hey."

"We need to talk."

"Okay. When?"

"What are you doing right now?"

"Homework."

"Can you meet me over at the park on Littleton?"

"Uh, sure."

"I'll see you there in fifteen minutes."

The line went dead. Benjamin stared down at it. What did Nathan want? A sense of dread crept into Benjamin's twisted gut.

Nathan was sitting on a park bench throwing pebbles at a sapling when Benjamin arrived. A slight breeze carried the smell of roses blooming in a nearby flower garden.

"What's up?" asked Benjamin, carefully.

Nathan took a minute to answer. Benjamin waited patiently.

"I've been running that car crash around in my head every day. I can't understand what happened. The car should've hit that girl."

"Emily."

"What?" Nathan looked up slightly annoyed at the interruption.

"Her name is Emily."

"Whatever. Anyways, what I've been trying to figure out is how it flew the other way into that wall."

Benjamin was staring at his feet. It was something he liked to do when he felt uncomfortable. Both boys were silent as the last comment hung in the air.

"Maybe it's like my mom said. Maybe it just swerved at the last second."

Nathan shook his head. "No. I've been around cars my whole life and I've never heard of something like that happening. I even asked my dad and he said the same thing. He said the only thing that could do something like that was a tornado or hurricane. We don't get those around here."

Again the silence. Nathan grabbed another pebble and threw it at a squirrel that happened to be running by. The animal screeched and scurried away in search of a human free zone.

"So why have you been ignoring me?" Benjamin asked cautiously.

"I don't know. First it was the thing at school where you pushed me. I know that was my fault, but the car crash made me think about it again. How did you push me…or hit me that hard? Then there was the car thing. I don't know what to think."

Nathan picked up a fistful of pebbles and chucked them all at the same time. His face contorted in anger.

"I don't know what you want me to say," said Benjamin.

"Tell me what's going on!" Nathan yelled.

Benjamin backed away a step. That made Nathan laugh.

"Don't worry. I learned my lesson. I won't be fighting you again."

Benjamin tried to smile, but he couldn't. Instead a weird grimace came to his face.

"Does that mean you won't tell me?" asked Nathan.

"I don't know what to tell you."

"You're lying." Nathan stood up and started to leave.

"I'm not lying," Benjamin pleaded. "I don't know what's going on either."

Nathan stared at his friend with a cold look in his eyes.

"You're the first friend I've had in a long time," Benjamin said quietly. "I don't want to mess that up."

The comment caught Nathan off guard. He paused as if rethinking his decision to walk home. Suddenly his eyes lit up.

"Wait a minute. You mean those weird things have never happened around you before?"

Benjamin shook his head.

"What if…"

"What?" Benjamin asked hopefully.

"What if you have…super powers?"

CHAPTER 9

PRACTICE MAKES PERFECT

Benjamin stood in shock. He'd be lying if he said he hadn't thought about it, especially after the pencil thing. But he didn't feel any different. Shouldn't he at least feel *something*?

"That's impossible," said Benjamin.

"Has anything else weird happened?"

"I don't think so," mumbled Benjamin. The look on his face gave him away.

"I thought so!" smiled Nathan, triumphantly.

Benjamin wanted to melt into the ground.

"So what was it? Did you fly in the air or stop time?" asked Nathan, his face a mask of unbridled curiosity.

"I…it was nothing, I think."

"Tell me, dude."

Benjamin finally looked up at the larger boy and told him the story about dropping the pencil in class.

"That's awesome!"

Benjamin smiled sheepishly, but then a look of dread replaced the grin.

"You can't tell anyone," pleaded Benjamin.

"Why not? This is gonna be so sweet!"

Benjamin fear-filled eyes stopped Nathan's exultation.

"What is it?"

Tears welled in Benjamin's eyes.

"What's wrong?" asked Nathan cautiously.

"I don't want to be a freak. They always make fun of me. I don't want it worse."

"Come on, it won't be that bad. You'll be so popular. Besides, if anyone tries to mess with you I'll take care of them."

He punched his palm with his fist. The *smack* almost made Benjamin jump.

"You have to promise me you won't tell anyone, Nathan."

Nathan Pratt stared at Benjamin with a stupid smirk.

"Fine," he said finally. "But I get to be your sidekick."

After swearing to keep the secret, the two boys spit into their hands and shook on it. Benjamin's secret was safe.

"So what should we try to do first?" Nathan asked excitedly.

Benjamin shrugged.

"I don't know how to do it."

"It's probably just like those movies. Concentrate on something really hard and make it move."

Nathan picked up a small brown rock and held it in his open hand.

"This should be easy. Try it!"

Benjamin looked around the park to see if anyone was watching. They were the only ones there.

Benjamin closed his eyes, took a deep breath, and tried to concentrate.

"Here goes..."

Benjamin tried to move the small rock for almost an hour. Sometimes he would just stand and stare at it, willing it to move. Other times he tried putting his hand about six inches above it. One time Nathan said he thought he felt something, but it turned out to be a breeze blowing through the deserted park.

"It's okay. Why don't we try again tomorrow?" suggested Nathan. "Here, catch."

The tiny rock lobbed its way toward Benjamin who wasn't expecting the throw. He moved to shield his face. Instead of hitting him, the stone stopped in midair, pivoted and rocketed back at Nathan.

"Ouch!" yelled Nathan, when the pebble pegged his chest.

Benjamin hadn't seen it.

"What happened?" he asked, frightened.

Nathan was rubbing his chest, but smiling.

"You did it."

"Did what?"

"The rock stopped in the air and flew back at me."

"I did that?" asked Benjamin, in shock.

"Yeah."

The huge grin on Nathan's face made Benjamin smile back. He looked down at his hand. It didn't look any different. There weren't any trails of smoke or scorch spots. Wasn't that how it worked in the movies?

"What were you thinking when you did it?" asked Nathan.

"I don't know. I guess I didn't want it to hit my face."

Nathan snapped his fingers.

"Have you ever heard about how people get like super strength and stuff when there's an emergency?"

"You mean like when a dad lifts a whole car off his kids or something?"

"Yeah! Maybe you're doing the same thing."

"I don't know, Nathan. It doesn't make me feel any different. I think I remember reading that when that happens it's all adrenaline."

"So?"

"So when it's over the person feels really tired. I don't feel tired or anything."

"Hmmm. Maybe your powers are just stronger. Maybe you won't get drained."

They could've kept talking about theories but Nathan's cell phone rang in his pocket. He pulled it out.

"It's my mom. Shoot. I better go. Try again tomorrow after school?"

Benjamin nodded.

"Cool. See ya, Dragon!"

Benjamin watched him go. He'd told the truth. He didn't feel any different. Maybe a little scared. What if his weird powers hurt someone? What if they happened when he didn't want? What if someone found out? What if his parents found out?

As he turned and walked home, Benjamin Dragon vowed to not let his parents or anyone other than Nathan know. He didn't want to be freak.

A small part of his mind started to think about the possibilities. What would his powers let him do?

CHAPTER 10

THE NOTE

Over the next few days Benjamin and Nathan spent every afternoon together. Sometimes they would go to the park and other days they would go to one of their houses.

They called it their 'practice.' The whole throw-something-at-Benjamin thing didn't work much. Benjamin suspected that it was because he wasn't surprised anymore. He knew Nathan was throwing a ball, a Cheeto or a stick at him.

Their practices got shorter and shorter as Benjamin's gift seemed to disappear.

"Maybe your brain's just tired," said Nathan one day.

"Maybe."

Benjamin didn't like disappointing his friend, but part of him was almost relieved. Sure it was cool to have a special gift, but he couldn't shake the fear that he might hurt some-one without even knowing it.

On their last day of practice, Benjamin finally mustered the courage to bring up the subject with Nathan.

"What do you think would happen if someone got hurt?" asked Benjamin.

"What do you mean?" asked Nathan whose mouth was full of puffy Cheetos. It was one of the perks of coming to Benjamin's house. His parents let him eat anything since he was so skinny.

"What if I accidently hurt someone with my power? I've already given you bruises three times."

Nathan thought about the question as he continued to shove the cheesy snacks in his mouth.

"We'll keep practicing until you can control it. Don't be such a worry wart."

Benjamin wasn't sure he could control it. He hadn't yet.

The next day at school was just like any other. Benjamin opened his dinged blue locker to get his brown bag before lunch. His mom still liked to pack it for him. Benjamin didn't mind. She always bought him expensive organic food from the only specialty store in town. Mrs. Dragon thought it would make him healthier.

Benjamin's friends gave him a hard time about the bagged lunch until they saw what was inside. They always wanted to trade. So instead of his packed lunch, Benjamin would always have an ample supply of school cafeteria pizza, french fries and ice cream. He liked it better anyway and it made him look a little cooler in the eyes of his new friends. Sometimes they fought over who got what. It was pretty funny. That way he kept his mom and his friends happy. He was happy too.

As he reached to the back of his locker for his food, Benjamin noticed a weathered note taped to the inside of the locker door. It was folded neatly and his name was printed on the outside in beautiful calligraphy.

Benjamin glanced around. Was someone playing a trick on him? He nervously tore the note from the tape. The paper felt old and heavy. Its edges were a dull brown.

He opened the folded note and almost dropped it in fright. Inside, in the same neat handwriting, it said:

I know. Meet me in your backyard after school.

Benjamin shook as he read the note three times, four times, five times. He probably would've cried if he hadn't been so scared. Shoving the note in his pocket, he closed the locker and headed to the cafeteria.

His face was pale gray when he sat down. The other boys had their lunches, but had waited to see what Benjamin had in his brown bag.

"Where's your lunch?" asked Little Mikey. Despite his small size he somehow always ate more than anyone else.

"I call dibs on your dessert!" said Funny Paul, making a face that looked like a rabid dog.

Only Nathan seemed to notice the look on Benjamin's face.

"What's wrong?" asked Nathan.

"I...I'm not hungry."

"Feeling okay?"

"I'll be fine. I think I ate something funny this morning." Benjamin grabbed his stomach to show them. "My mom made me some goat cheese omelettes."

The other boys made faces.

"Gross!" said Funny Paul.

"Nasty!" said Little Mikey.

Everyone except Nathan dug into their food now that they wouldn't be able to trade with Benjamin. Nathan scooted closer and whispered, "Are you sure you're okay?" He knew Benjamin's looks. They'd gotten to know each other well. Nathan sensed that something wasn't right.

"I'm alright. I think I'm gonna go see the nurse."

"Want me to come?"

Benjamin shook his head. "No. I don't want you to see me if I puke." He forced a tiny smile on his face and got up from the table.

Nathan watched him go, his face furrowed with concern.

Benjamin stayed in the nurse's office for the rest of the school day. She said there didn't seem to be anything wrong with him, but even she couldn't ignore the pale face and sweaty palms.

"Maybe I'll feel better if I just lay here for a while," suggested Benjamin.

"I think I'd better call your mom, Benjamin. Maybe she can take you to the doctor."

"No! I mean, I have Mrs. O'Brian for last period and she's giving a quiz. I don't want to…uh, miss it."

The nurse shook her head and smiled warmly. "I wish all of our students were as serious about their school work as you, Benjamin. Okay then, why don't you take a little nap and I'll come check on you every half hour or so."

She winked and patted him on the head. There were perks to being a good kid in school. Teachers tended to believe you if you were smart and not getting in trouble.

Benjamin tried to close his eyes, but the note in his pocket seemed to be burning a hole in his brain.

I know. Meet me in your backyard after school.

Should he tell someone? Should he bring Nathan? Who could know? How could anyone else know about his powers?

Benjamin's mind whirled with possibilities.

CHAPTER 11

THE VISITOR

After school, Benjamin told Nathan that he had a lot of homework to do and wouldn't be able to hang out. Besides, he still wasn't feeling well and looked the part with his sunken eyes and pale skin.

"Hope you feel better. See you tomorrow," Nathan waved as he boarded the school bus.

Benjamin waved back and sighed. The walk home would give him some time to think. Maybe whoever had left him the note would be gone. Maybe the person was waiting for the school bus and would leave when Benjamin didn't get off at his stop. Maybe, maybe, maybe…

The walk home felt like forever and all too quick at the same time. Benjamin clutched his hands nervously as he walked. He barely paid attention to his surroundings as he moved on autopilot. That was, until a very old man with a gnarled wooden cane stepped out in front of him.

Benjamin went to move around the man, but stopped. He didn't stop himself. He couldn't move his legs or arms. They were paralyzed. His head could move and he lifted it to look at the old man. The ancient white-haired man had a neatly trimmed beard and long hair that ran in two braids that cascaded over his shoulders. He was wearing some kind of brown suit, with a t-shirt underneath that said 'Live For Now'. There seemed to be a million wrinkles on the man's face and hands that were tanned and craggily. Benjamin inhaled sharply as he noticed the man's eyes. They were a brilliant blue-green, the color of the Caribbean Sea in the shallows around little islands. They shone and even looked a bit mischievous.

"You weren't thinking of avoiding me, were you, Benjamin?"

CHAPTER 12

LESSONS

Benjamin's mouth opened and closed with no words coming out. He looked like a bug-eyed fish that had just been surprised by a great white shark.

"I take it you got my note?" the old man said with a slightly European accent that you might here from someone who's lived all over the world. The man smiled from ear to ear. His teeth were a little crooked, but brilliantly clean like the insides of a seashell.

Somehow Benjamin managed to move his head up and down.

"Good. Are you hungry?"

"N…no, s…sir," Benjamin stuttered.

"Don't worry, my boy. I'm not here to hurt you. I'm here to help you!"

The look on Benjamin's face showed his reluctance to believe the stranger.

"It would be a lot easier if you did believe me and started talking," said the man.

"O…okay."

"Good!"

The bright-eyed visitor snapped his fingers and Benjamin's arms flopped down to his sides. He looked down at them in wonder.

"Let's go grab some ice cream," suggested the man.

Without turning to look back at Benjamin, he stepped off the curb and headed toward the town center. His step was as graceful as a cat's. It was interesting that the man carried a cane. He didn't look like he needed it. Maybe it was just an old man thing, like for decoration.

Once he'd gathered his wits, Benjamin followed.

Soon they arrived at the small ice cream shop run by a large man with a black beard. He looked like he would've been more at home in a pizzeria.

"What can I get for you?" the owner of the shop asked.

"I'll get a scoop of rainbow sherbet and a scoop of bubble gum," the old man ordered.

"And you, young man?"

"I...I'm okay."

"Benjamin will have chocolate fudge brownie please," said the man in the brown suit.

Benjamin looked up in shock. How had the stranger known his favorite ice cream? All he got in response was a quick wink from a wrinkle wrapped eye.

They waited in silence as their ice cream was scooped and served in matching white paper bowls. The man with the cane paid and ushered Benjamin to a small table next to the front window. They were the only customers in the shop. The owner told them he'd be in the back office doing paperwork if they needed anything else.

"I'm sure you have some questions for me, eh?" the man asked between bites of ice cream.

Benjamin nodded. He was finally starting to relax and enjoy his dessert.

"First, my name is Kennedy."

"Is that your first or your last name?" asked Benjamin.

The man shrugged. "It's the only name I can remember."

How could that be? Didn't everyone know their own name?

"Why do you only have one name?"

"I decided to live by one name a very long time ago, but that doesn't really matter. As I said earlier, I am here to help you."

"How, Mr. Kennedy?"

"Not Mr. Kennedy, just Kennedy."

"Oh." Benjamin face reddened. Kennedy didn't seem to notice.

"Where was I? Oh yes! Your gift."

"My what?"

"Don't give me that, Benjamin. I saw what you did with that car."

A sneaky grin spread across Kennedy's face.

"I don't know what you mean."

"You used your gift and saved that pretty young girl."

"No, I…I didn't…"

"Pish posh, son. Let's not lie to each other. You have a gift just as I do. I've admitted it to you. Can you do the same for me?"

"Yes, sir."

"That's better. Now, you must have some questions for me?"

Benjamin laid down his plastic spoon and wiped his mouth with a napkin. His stomach was in knots again. He was nervous, but curious. Benjamin wanted answers.

"Why do I..." Benjamin started.

Kennedy held up a gnarled hand.

"I forgot to tell you. One of my rules is that you only get three questions per visit. I'll hold you to it."

"Per visit?"

"Would you like to use one of your questions for me to answer that?"

Benjamin thought about it for a moment.

"Yes."

"Very well. From time to time, until I die, I will visit you. You'll never know when or where. You see, it's in my nature to be a little mysterious. We're all a little different. My good friend Annabelle prefers to live in trees and Unger wears... Woops. That's just like me to go off on a tangent. Must be my old brain." Kennedy tapped his head. "As I was saying, I'll show up sometimes to check on you and to help you along your chosen path. During those visits I will allow three questions about your ongoing quests, your path or your gift. Don't worry. You won't waste one asking to use the restroom!"

Benjamin's mouth hung open. Chosen path? Gifts? Quests?! What was this old man talking about? There were too many questions to ask. Why did he only get three? Benjamin's brain worked to come up with a better question.

"What are these gifts?" he asked quietly.

Kennedy tapped his nose with his spoon. "There are those in the human race that possess certain talents. Some people might call them powers. I prefer to use the term gift. Has a better ring to it, I think. Having these talents is very rare. There are only a handful of us in the entire world, although that number seems to have increased recently...Our gifts are divided into three general categories: healing, growing, and destruction. One who is imbued with the gift of healing is able to heal and affect the physical well-being of living creatures. Some world famous doctors and healers have had this gift. Quite a serious lot if you ask me.

"Those with the gift of growing possess the ability to manipulate the earth and our environment. For example, they can make a tiny acorn sprout into a ten-foot-tall tree or make a cloud expel rain. Extremely useful when you want to grow a garden in a pinch. Growers tend to be our gentlest souls."

Kennedy paused to eat another bite of rainbow sherbet. He was more serious as he began again.

"The gift of destruction is more loosely defined. I call it destruction, others call it control and liken it to telekinesis, the power to move objects and manipulate the physical world. I, however, find that using the term 'destruction' properly warns us of the gift's...side effects. You see, those who have gone astray have almost always had the gift of destruction. Very sad when that happens."

Benjamin's faced turned gray.

"I have the gift of destruction, although I use my gift for good." He smiled. "One of the reasons I am here today is that we believed you had, and I have now seen, that you have the same gift. I am to be your mentor of sorts. Final question?"

Healing. Growing. Destruction! It was almost too much for Benjamin to process. He didn't want to be one of the bad guys. It was hard enough trying to be good!

"Why do we have these gifts? Who gave them to us?" asked Benjamin, all thoughts of chocolate fudge ice cream swept from his mind.

"Technically that was two questions, but I'll treat it as one I suppose. Although I'm not sure you'll like the answer."

Kennedy pursed his lips, thinking.

"We don't know where our gifts come from. Each of us has our own theories. Some say it's God, some say it may be something else. I, honestly, have never been too sure. Either way, most of us are in agreement as to WHY we have these gifts. It is generally thought that gifted individuals exist in order to bring balance to the world. That may seem a bit grandiose, but once you think about it, it makes sense. That brings me back to an earlier thought. I mentioned we've seen a slight uptick in the number of our newly gifted. I'm sure if you watch the news you see the problems all over the world. It's as if nature is correcting itself. The same thing happened during the Second World War. As far as we can determine, the World War Two era birthed the most gifted in our long history. There were upwards of one hundred of us. I was in Europe at the time. Nasty business. Saw some horrible things…" Kennedy's voice trailed off and his eyes clouded for a moment.

"Ahem," Kennedy cleared his throat in his hand. "Today there are close to twenty of us, and likely more to come."

Benjamin's mind swirled. It all sounded too farfetched. He wished he could pinch himself to make sure he was really still awake.

"That brings us back to you, Benjamin. You're still a bit young for questing and whatnot. That does not mean you cannot start thinking about your chosen path. I can see I've confused you again."

Benjamin nodded and Kennedy scratched his beard.

"Let's see. How to describe it? A chosen path is exactly as it sounds. For example, some healers set their minds to becoming doctors because they can use their gifts in a more public way. More on that in a minute.

"Many Growers live in the wild and cultivate magnificent forests and habitats for animals. There is a particularly talented gentleman by the name of Esteban who is doing extraordinary work in the Amazon. He's reviving the decimated rainforest. I'd love to see him at his craft if it weren't so bloody hot down there.

"What about destructors?" Benjamin interrupted.

Kennedy glared at his pupil for a moment, reminding Benjamin of one of his 2nd Grade teachers, Mrs. Graverton. She had a talent for making kids cry.

"I'll let the extra question pass because you're new. We destructors are the most varied in our chosen path. I suppose I could be a very effective builder, or some such thing. I'm almost sure there was a destructor involved with the construction of the great pyramids in Egypt. Regardless, we destructors are what you might call the wild card of our kind. There are fewer of us. We fit in where needed. I've devoted my life to travelling and helping during times of war or natural emergencies. I'm quite skilled at removing debris after hurricanes. It also allows me to spend time on beautiful islands in the Caribbean."

Benjamin liked the sound of that.

"Another destructor I know is sort of a vigilante, meaning he helps the police catch criminals. He's quite good at it. I once helped him nab a gang of crooks in the middle of a bank theft. You should have seen the looks on their faces!"

Kennedy finished his ice cream and held up his spoon.

"Now, my warning for you as a fellow destructor. I already told you that destructors have the largest chance of going down the wrong path."

Kennedy let go of the plastic spoon. Instead of landing on the table it hung in the air. Benjamin gawked open-mouthed once again.

"I want you to remember that you have the power of destruction." Kennedy stared keenly into Benjamin's eyes. "Watch the spoon."

Benjamin watched as the spoon started spinning slowly in the space between them. Its momentum picked up and it was soon only a whirl of white blowing a miniscule amount of air at Benjamin's face.

There were no squints or hand motions from the older man. He merely stared at Benjamin.

Without warning the spoon halted in midair and began folding on itself. It made a tiny crackling sound as if it were screaming. It crumpled into a ball. Kennedy reached out and snagged the balled spoon.

"This is the danger of our gift, Benjamin. There are no limits to our power. We must use it wisely."

Benjamin's face had gone from a gray to creamy white.

"It's not as bad as all that!" exclaimed Kennedy. "I just wanted to make sure you understood the possible conse-quences." He snapped his fingers and his white eyebrows rose. Benjamin jumped in his chair. "I almost forgot! The rules."

Benjamin looked at his teacher quizzically.

"The rules?" he asked.

"Yes. I cannot believe I almost forgot about them. I get so caught up in the stories sometimes you know…Any-who, let me tell you about the rules. The most important rule is to not tell an un-gifted person about your talents. Could you imagine what could happen? The way the media is these days they would turn us into travelling circuses. Worse, someone could use you for their own gain. It is, therefore, imperative that you keep your gift a secret. Understood?"

Benjamin's face had colored. He hoped Kennedy didn't have the power to read his mind. Instead of commenting, Kennedy went on.

"Second, you must use your gift for good. You do not want to see what happens to one of us that go astray. I'll just say that the rest of us don't take kindly to it, and we will do anything we can to protect our world.

"Third, even though we may be gifted, we are still mortal. That means we can still die and get hurt. Our gifts don't change that."

Benjamin waited for more rules. None came.

Kennedy rose to leave just as the fat parlor owner emerged from the back office.

"Until we meet again, Benjamin. Practice your craft, be careful and think on your chosen path."

Kennedy offered his hand and Benjamin stood to shake it.

"Thank you for coming Mr...err...Kennedy."

The old man's smile was contagious.

"You are most welcome, my boy."

He released Benjamin's hand and headed to the exit, cane swinging jauntily at his side. Just as he opened the glass door and the chime sounded, Kennedy turned back.

"I almost forgot. One last thing. I really must have Imelda scan me again. It wouldn't do to have Alzheimer's as a destructor..." he muttered to himself. "This has only happened once in the past three or so thousand years, but every once in a while a truly gifted individual comes along. That person possesses all three gifts. You may have heard of one that graced our world around two thousand years ago," he said with a wink. "Not something you should worry about, but we feel it's important to let all newly gifted know in the extremely off chance that you start developing healing or growing gifts as well. Could come as quite a fright!"

With that he departed and disappeared around the corner. Benjamin stood still for a full minute.

"You okay, son?" asked the store owner.

"Uh...yes, sir. Just...uh, had too much ice cream I think," lied Benjamin.

CHAPTER 13

WHAT NOW?

Benjamin sat in his tidy room staring out the window. He'd replayed the conversation with Kennedy over and over in his head. There had also been a lot of painful pinches to make sure he was still awake.

It was almost dark and his mom would be home soon. Mrs. Dragon had texted to tell him she'd be bringing home Chinese food for dinner. Benjamin wasn't hungry.

Kennedy's warnings and instructions echoed in his head. He knew he could have asked questions for weeks, if given the chance. Why did he only get three? There were so many things he wanted to learn. How should he practice? Where should he practice? How was he supposed to find his chosen path? What if he ran into another one of the gifted? What if he became one of 'bad' gifted? Was there a better name to call them than 'gifted'?

His head pounded from the strain. Benjamin wished he could talk to someone about it. Would it be better if they teamed him up with someone like when his dad had made him play soccer in third grade?

Only ten years old, Benjamin was scared. He was scared of doing something wrong. He was scared of not knowing what to do. He was scared of someone finding out. He was scared of being weird, a freak.

Benjamin heard the garage door creaking open. It was his mom coming home. His dad was out of town again on business.

He ran to the bathroom and threw some cold water on his face. Benjamin's mom was usually too preoccupied with work stuff to realize when something was going on with her son, but he didn't want to take the chance. His nerves were already frazzled. His plan was to eat a little bit and then say he had a lot of homework to do. That wasn't unusual.

Benjamin dried his face on bath towel and took a deep breath.

"Calm down," he said to himself.

He really shouldn't have worried. After giving him a quick hug and the bag of Chinese food, Mrs. Dragon left the kitchen to get on a conference call. Benjamin picked at his food for a couple minutes until he gave up and went upstairs.

Too exhausted to think, Benjamin flopped onto his bed and fell asleep.

Benjamin woke to his mom shaking him.

"Wake up, Benji. Wake up. Are you okay?" Mrs. Dragon asked. She was in her nightgown and her eyes looked heavy from sleep.

"What's wrong, mom?" Benjamin groaned.

"You were shouting in your sleep, honey. I heard you all the way in my room." The master bedroom was on the opposite side of the house on the first level.

Worry creased her normally serene face.

"I'm okay, mom. I…I guess I was just having a dream."

"Why are you still in your clothes and why is your light on?"

"I guess I was more tired than I thought. Fell asleep in my clothes," he shrugged and croaked a laugh.

Mrs. Dragon shook her head.

"I keep telling you to get more sleep, honey. Are you sure you're okay?"

"I'm fine, mom."

She looked at him for a moment.

"I'll leave your door open. If you need to come sleep with me, just come downstairs."

"Mom!"

She put her hands up in surrender. "Okay, okay. But I'm leaving the door open."

Benjamin rolled his eyes as Mrs. Dragon made her way back to bed. He laid his head on his pillow and draped an arm over his eyes.

What had he been dreaming about? He couldn't remember.

———◆———

The next morning Benjamin got up early and packed his books for school. He was anxious to get back to where things were normal. Normal? Would anything ever be normal again?

———•—•———

Nathan found him at his locker minutes before the bell.

"Hey, you feeling better?" Nathan asked.

Benjamin flashed a forced smile.

"I'm okay. I think I was just tired."

"Good, cuz I was thinking that maybe.." Nathan looked around and lowered his voice to a whisper, "maybe we can go over to the park and practice again."

"I don't know. I've got a lot of homework to do tonight."

"Come on, dude. I know it doesn't take you long to finish. Just for a little bit, okay?"

Before Benjamin could reply, the school bell rang and they both ran to their first class of the day.

———•—•———

The two friends didn't have any classes together in the morning. Benjamin spent his first three classes half paying attention to the lessons and half trying to figure out how he'd get out of going to the park with Nathan. Old Kennedy (that's what Benjamin had decided to privately call his mentor) had been clear about keeping his gift secret.

Now that he thought about it, Benjamin was sure that his nightmare had something to do with the other gifted people coming to punish him after they found out that Nathan knew about his gift. Benjamin imagined shapes peeking in through the pollen encrusted school windows. He needed to come up with an excuse for his friend.

———

Lunchtime came and went. Benjamin traded away the food his mother had packed, but only picked at the mound of french fries he'd gotten in return. He hadn't eaten a whole meal since breakfast the day before. Benjamin wondered if it was possible to starve to death from worry. The thought made him shove another ketchup and mustard covered fry into his mouth.

His friends jabbered on like nothing had happened. They were used to Benjamin keeping to himself. The only times he actively participated in lunch conversations was when they needed his brain. He liked feeling needed. This time, however, he just wanted to hide in a corner.

Nathan glanced at him a couple times and Benjamin forced a smile back. It was going to be a long day.

———

After school, Nathan convinced Benjamin to walk home. They'd stop at the park on the way. Benjamin kept tight-lipped as Nathan went on about some girl in 8th grade.

"What about you?" Nathan's question momentarily woke Benjamin from his stupor.

"Huh?"

"I asked if you like any girls in our class."

Benjamin blushed at the comment. Being two years younger than his classmates not only meant that he was shorter than everyone (except that nice kid Salvatore in the wheelchair), it also meant he had to listen to his friends go on and on about girls. It wasn't that Benjamin didn't like girls. He turned pink every time he saw Emily. Being naturally shy only made it worse when he tried to talk to older girls. They looked at him like a little brother or something. It was easy for Nathan. He was already taller than most of the 8th grade boys and he could talk to anyone.

"Not me."

"Well maybe if Mandy says yes to going out…"

Nathan's voice trailed off as his gaze fixated ahead.

"There she is!" Nathan whispered.

Benjamin followed his friend's eyes. A few yards away two girls walked toward them.

"Quick, how does my hair look?" Nathan asked.

"Uh, fine I…"

"Do you have a piece of gum?"

Benjamin couldn't help laughing. He'd never seen Nathan act this way.

"What?" asked Nathan.

"I'm…uh, all out of gum. Sorry."

"Okay. Shh."

The girls were fifty feet away when they noticed Benjamin and Nathan.

"Hi, Mandy!" Nathan waved.

The girl with the light brown hair sighed. "Hello, Nathan."

Nathan didn't seem to notice the tone of annoyance in Mandy's voice.

"Where are you guys going?"

Both girls looked down at Benjamin and giggled. Mandy whispered something into her friend's ear. They giggled again.

Nathan's face colored as he realized that they were laughing at his friend. Benjamin dropped his gaze to the pavement.

"What's so funny?" Nathan's smile disappeared.

"Oh, nothing. Cynthia was just wondering where you found your midget."

The girls started laughing so hard it looked like they might start crying in hysteria. Benjamin was too embarrassed to say anything. Nathan wasn't. His voice came out like a striking whip.

"You shut up!"

Mandy and Cynthia stopped laughing and looked at Nathan warily. He was quivering with anger.

Instead of apologizing they crossed the street and resumed their whispers and giggles.

Nathan put a hand on Benjamin's shoulder. "I'm sorry, Benjamin. They shouldn't have said that. Don't worry I won't ask her out."

When the smaller boy looked up there were tears in his eyes.

"Come on, man, let's go to the park," suggested Nathan.

Benjamin shook his head. "I think I'll just go home."

Nathan nodded and pulled his hand back.

"I'm sorry."

"It's not your fault. I'll see you tomorrow."

Leaving Nathan standing where they'd stopped, Benjamin forced himself to continue on. Nothing had changed.

CHAPTER 14

RESEARCH

Benjamin did his best to avoid his friends until the weekend. It wasn't hard. The only class he had with them at school was P.E. He spent his lunches in the library working on a fake research paper.

What he was really doing was searching for any clue about his gift. Benjamin quickly found that the middle school library didn't have much in the way of heavy reading. Instead, he used the internet to scour websites for any sign of humans with powers.

First he looked at sites talking about magic wands and witches. He soon ignored those. Kennedy hadn't said anything about using a wand much less a broomstick. Silly.

After that he typed in 'magic'. The definitions varied. More professional sites like Wikipedia mentioned incantations or spells. That still didn't sound right to Benjamin. He hadn't said anything to stop Nathan, pick up the pencil or save Emily. Benjamin did find the word 'paranormal'. He clicked on the link.

It broke down 'paranormal' into two parts: 'para' and 'normal'. 'Para' in latin meant above, outside or beyond. That sounded pretty spot on to Benjamin. 'Paranormal' basically meant 'outside normal'. He almost laughed out loud. That sounded like a perfect word to describe his life before he'd found out about his freaky destruction gift.

"Paranormal," he said out loud.

A group of eight graders looked up at his unconscious blurt.

"Shhh!" said one of the girls.

"Sorry," whispered Benjamin. Trying to ignore the annoyed glares, he refocused on the computer screen.

At the bottom of the webpage he found another word: Psionics. He clicked on the link. Psionics was described as using the mind to do paranormal things like moving objects and reading minds.

Next he looked for anything mentioning miracles or unexplained events. There was a lot about Area 51 and psychics telling fortunes. For a second Benjamin wondered if maybe he should go see a fortune teller. No. He'd be in big trouble if the fortune teller found out about his gift.

Benjamin huffed in frustration and went to click out of the website. His hand slipped and he accidentally clicked on another link titled 'Hurricane Katrina'.

"Oops."

He waited for the slow library computer to load the page. It finally came up. There was an article. At the top was a picture of a black family huddled together, smiling at the camera. Benjamin quickly read the short story.

BENJAMIN DRAGON - AWAKENING

Miracle In The Midst of Misery

Hurricane Katrina ravaged the Gulf Coast leaving thousands stranded and homeless. There are many stories of death and destruction. This is not one of them. Amidst the misery in the aftermath of the powerful storm we found examples of hope and possibly even miracles.

Ina Johnson, a single mother of five and long-time resident of New Orleans, made the fateful decision to remain in her neighborhood home during the hurricane. It wasn't until too late, when the water had already risen over five feet inside their home, that the Johnsons attempted to evacuate.

"None of my kids can swim," said Ms. Johnson. "We held on to each other, the older boys helping the younger ones. I prayed and prayed that God would deliver us..."

With the entire neighborhood flooded, the family tried to make it to a major highway. They never made it. The Johnsons glimpsed the still lit road ahead. Ms. Johnson remembers, "All of a sudden the water started rising real fast."

What she couldn't have known was that not minutes before, the levy nearest their location broke, allowing massive amounts of seawater to enter. This fact, along with the timeline, was confirmed with the Army Corps of Engineers.

Illuminated by the streets lights Ina Johnson stared in horror as an enormous wave barreled down on her family.

"I said, 'Oh, God, please save my babies."

*According to Ms. Johnson, Instead of the being pum-
meled by the roaring water, the wave parted. That isn't the
most amazing part of the story. She then says her entire
family lifted into the air and touched down gently on a
five-story building a block away. The family was safe.
"We was flyin'," said twelve-year-old Ronald Johnson.
"I neva' knew we could do that," remarked
eight-year-old Stevie Johnson.
So what really happened? We might never know. This
reporter has confirmed that the building in question
was, in fact, completely boarded up prior to Hurricane
Katrina making landfall. There also aren't any ladders
to allow a normal person to climb up the building.
"It was a miracle, I tell ya," says Ina Johnson.
We might never know what really happened on that dark night
in September. Was it a miracle? What we do know is that
the Ina Johnson and her family will live on to tell their tale.*

Benjamin stared at the computer screen. Hadn't Old
Kennedy told him that he'd chosen to help out during storms
and stuff? Could that have been him or someone else with a gift?

Looking around for another blue link, Benjamin found
one labeled 'Hurricane Hugo'. The page pulled up another
story similar to the one told about Hurricane Katrina. This
time it was about a man and his dog. The man had decided to
ride out the storm. His house had collapsed and he'd somehow escaped the devastation. It said Hurricane Hugo hit the
southeast U.S. in 1989.

Benjamin scratched his head. Were they just two random events? That's when he noticed a name listed in the reference block: *Jarvis Mandry*. He was the one who'd found the separate articles and compiled them for the website. Benjamin clicked on the man's name.

The next page outlined Mr. Mandry's background. He was a paranormal investigator with degrees from the University of Virginia, Yale and Stanford. Mr. Mandry became a writer in the early 1980s although he was still conducting investigations into unusual events.

Benjamin scrolled down the page and his jaw dropped. There were over one hundred links to articles about unexplained events and supposed miracles. Benjamin scanned the titles.

'Baby Survives Six Story Drop'
'Woman Miraculously Cured After Being
Diagnosed With 73 Tumors'
'Rebirth of a Once Dead Forest'
'Man Regains Sight After Being Blind for 37 Years'

The stories went on and on.

"Hey!"

Benjamin jumped at the sound of Nathan's voice behind him.

"What are you working on?"

Benjamin closed the internet browser and looked up.

"I...uh, just doing some research for a paper."

"Shhh!" hissed the group two tables away.

Nathan rolled his eyes at them and motioned for them to mind their own business. They did as commanded. Nathan was still one of the biggest boys in school and popular. Most people listened to him.

"Did you already eat?" asked Nathan.

"Yeah."

"Cool. I just wanted to come check on you. You've been quiet."

Benjamin smiled at the comment. He appreciated someone worrying about him. Unfortunately he now carried a burden only he could know about.

"Just busy, but thanks."

"Wanna hang out after school?"

"I've really got…"

"I know, I know. You've got a lot of homework. How about I come over to your place and bring my homework. I won't bug you, I promise."

He made a funny face that almost made it seem like he was begging.

"Uh, sure."

"Awesome! I'll meet you on the bus."

Benjamin watched his friend walk away. Maybe he needed a little company. Being alone always made his mind wander too much.

CHAPTER 15

SUMMER CAMP

Benjamin and Nathan sat next to each other on the bus. Nathan wanted to talk about girls. Benjamin kept steering the conversation back to things like video games and new movies.

"I can't believe we only have a couple more weeks of school. I'm sooo ready for summer," said Nathan, sweeping a hand through his hair. "What are you doing this summer?"

"I don't know. I think my parents want me to go to some camp. Camp Waha…"

"Camp Wahamalican?!"

"Uh, I think so."

"You lucky turd. That place is awesome," crowed Nathan. "Have you gone?"

"Me? No way. My parents can't afford it." For one of the few times since Benjamin had known him, Nathan's face colored.

"Well, I don't even know if I'm going. I think I'd rather stay home."

"No way, Dragon!" Nathan had recently taken to calling Benjamin by his last name. He said it sounded cooler. "There's so much stuff to do. Plus, it's half girls!"

Once again Benjamin shifted the conversation to something more comfortable. "What do they do at Camp Wahamachooky?"

"Wahamalican. It's like all the outdoor stuff you want. Camping, fishing, hiking, canoeing, archery...Man, I've wanted to go there forever. I think Aaron's going this year."

Benjamin loved being outside. The only thing he didn't like was mosquitoes. They always seemed to find him first. His mom called him the family Mosquito Magnet. He wished Nathan could go with him. At least he'd know Aaron. Maybe he could find his chosen path at camp.

Benjamin could only fake doing homework for so long. So after finishing all his assignments the two boys played video games. They were thrashing the enemy in *Call of Duty* when Nathan's cell phone rang.

"It's my mom. Can you pause the game?"

Benjamin pressed pause and waited.

"Hey, mom. Yeah, I'm over at the Dragon's." He looked up at Benjamin and mimed eating. He was asking if it was okay to stay and eat. Benjamin knew his parents wouldn't care. They barely paid attention to him at dinner anyway. Besides, Mr. Dragon was out of town again. Benjamin nodded and Nathan smiled.

"Is it okay if I stay here for dinner?" Nathan asked his mom. He listened to her response and moaned, "Come on, mom. We always eat dinner together."

Mrs. Pratt finally relented and Nathan hung up the phone. Benjamin looked at his friend suspiciously. He'd never heard Nathan avoid his parents.

"What?" Nathan asked, noticing the look.

"Nothing. You ready to play?"

"Yeah. Let's win this mission, Sergeant Dragon."

Nathan thanked Mrs. Dragon for dinner and left out the back door. Benjamin was still pushing penne pasta around his plate.

"Hey, mom?"

"Yes, honey?" Mrs. Dragon kept her eyes glued to her work. She'd already finished her nightly salad.

"Do you still want me to go to that camp this summer?"

The question perked his mom's attention and she fixed him with a wary look. "Your father and I talked about it and we think it would be good for you."

Parents were always telling their kids what was good for them. What was that all about? Did they give the same class to all parents?

"Well...I was thinking that..."

Mrs. Dragon interrupted. "Come on, Benji. I know you don't like this kind of stuff, but..."

"Wait, mom. I was just gonna say that I think I want to go."

Mrs. Dragon's look of surprise almost made Benjamin laugh. Not many things surprised his mom.

"That's a welcome change. How about we talk about it with your dad this weekend?"

Benjamin nodded. "I was wondering if...I just..."

"What did you want to ask me, honey?" Mrs. Dragon looked like she didn't want the good news to stop. She rarely had anything in common with her son. There were so many things she wanted him to do. It was a delicate balancing act with Benjamin. She knew how smart he was, and yet he didn't possess the same confidence that his parent's had at his age.

"I know it's a lot to ask, mom, but I was wondering if we might be able to pay for Nathan to go to."

"That's very sweet, but I'm not sure the Pratts would allow it, Benji."

"Why not?"

"Some people are very sensitive about money. They might feel like they owed us. Mr. and Mrs. Pratt are the kind of people that work very hard for what they have and…" she struggled to find the words, "…they don't like taking or borrowing money from people."

"What if we just said it was a gift, mom?" The idea brought a smile to his face. "Yeah. If we said it was a gift then they couldn't feel bad. Didn't you tell me that people should be grateful when they get a gift? That's what you told me when I got that sweater with the pig on it from grandma."

Mrs. Dragon looked uncomfortable. She was in unfamiliar territory. On one hand, Benjamin was a good kid and never asked for anything. Mr. Dragon almost had to drag him to the mall to buy his Xbox. On the other hand, her lawyer brain was being outmatched by the wit of her son.

She groaned. "Let me talk to your dad. I'm not promising anything."

Benjamin hopped up from his chair, ran around the table and gave his mom a big kiss on the cheek. "Thanks, mom!"

CHAPTER 16

PLANS

After discussions with Mr. Dragon and Mr. and Mrs. Pratt, it was decided that the Dragons would pay for Nathan to go to Camp Wahamalican with Benjamin. Mr. Pratt insisted that it was only a loan and that Nathan would work off the debt over the rest of the summer and possibly the coming school year. Benjamin figured that his parents probably wouldn't take the money. They were different than he was, but they were always kind and generous.

Nathan practically bounced off the walls when Benjamin told him. He crushed his friend in a tight bear hug until he realized what he was doing, and promptly dropped Benjamin to the ground. Benjamin didn't care. He was glad to see his friend so happy.

———

The remaining weeks of school flew. Benjamin got straight A's for the millionth time in his life.

The three boys, Benjamin, Nathan and Aaron, carefully planned out their camping adventure. They would have three whole weeks away from home. Funny Paul and Little Mikey looked on. Both were a bit jealous. Funny Paul would be spending the summer at his grandparents' farm in Michigan. Little Mikey was going to soccer camp. He was already a really good player.

"We have to make sure we all get in the same cabin," Nathan declared. "If anyone tried to split us up…"

"I definitely want to take fishing. Tommy Hiller told me they have bass the size of a car in the lake," said the normally quiet Aaron.

Benjamin was just along for the ride. He was happy because his friends were happy. There hadn't even been any nightmares since finding out about camp. Every time he started to worry about his 'gift' he would dive into one of his books about snakes or bears to distract himself. And it worked. Because of camp, Benjamin never thought about Old Kennedy and having to find his 'chosen path'. Camp Wahamalican would change that.

CHAPTER 17

OFF TO CAMP WAHAMALICAN

The morning of the first day of camp came after a whirlwind of shopping and packing. Mrs. Dragon and Mrs. Pratt drove Benjamin and Nathan the three hours to Camp Wahamalican. Aaron's parents would be taking him separately. They'd already agreed to meet up at the large camp totem pole with the red eagle on top after dropping their stuff at the cabin.

Along the way, Nathan did most of the talking as they went through the camp brochures for the thousandth time.

"Everybody says we need to get to the chow hall early," Nathan was saying. "If we don't all the good food will be gone. Did I tell you about…"

And so it went for the three hour trip. Benjamin enjoyed every minute. Nathan was an animated story-teller and had lots of tales to tell about so-and-so camper being attacked by a wolverine or so-and-so camper getting poison ivy all over their private parts. Benjamin laughed even though he'd heard the stories before. He was glad Nathan was coming to camp.

When they arrived at Camp Wahamalican, registration was in full swing. Campers lined up with their parents to find out which tribe they'd be assigned to. Benjamin and Nathan were assigned to the Tomahawk tribe despite Benjamin being younger. Mrs. Dragon had somehow persuaded camp staff to allow the change in procedure do to the fact that Benjamin was two grades ahead of the kids his age. Benjamin figured that his mom had probably used some of her own powers to convince the camp director to let the two boys be in the same tribe.

After they'd paid for the camp store credit (Mrs. Pratt insisted she pay for Nathan's), gotten their camp T-shirts, and picked up their activities list, the Dragons and the Pratts made their way to the Tomahawk cabin. The slightly musty log cabin was a bustle of activity. Kids and parents hurried this way and that. One boy was crying as he said goodbye to his mother. Benjamin promised himself he would not cry.

Nathan threw his bags on a top bunk and said he'd unpack later. Benjamin took the bed below Nathan and followed his friend's lead. There would be plenty of time to put their things away. The boys were excited to go exploring.

They said goodbye to their moms (Mrs. Pratt started crying when she hugged Nathan). Benjamin's eyes got a little watery, but he didn't cry. After waving to their parents, Benjamin and Nathan headed to the tallest manmade object in camp: the Camp Wahamalican totem pole.

They found Aaron at the totem pole. He was leafing through the class brochure for wilderness survival. It said something about making a shelter out of branches and stuff.

"Let's go check out the lake," said Nathan.

They made their way through the tree lined path that they knew would open up to the lake. Benjamin had almost memorized the camp's layout as had the others. It was nice to walk in the shade and avoid the buzzing horse flies. They were anxious to see the biggest attraction at Camp Wahamalican.

Walking out into the sunlight the three friends stopped. Nathan's eyes popped wide. Aaron's mouth hung open. Benjamin was speechless. The lake looked like a kid's fairy tale. Canoes and kayaks were neatly piled in wooden racks close to the water. A sandy beach that looked like it had been recently raked lay just ahead. In the water just beyond the beach was a large water playground covered in ladders, diving boards, and slides. There were three bouncy inflatables tethered to the play center with ropes.

"Wow!" Nathan exclaimed, and took off running for the beach. The other two followed. Benjamin was admiring the view when they heard a whistle blow. All three boys skidded to a stop and looked for the whistle-blower.

Walking toward them was a tall blonde camp counselor. She looked to be in high school and had freckles painting a pattern under her eyes and over her nose. She was athletic and pretty. A brief whiff of sweet perfume accompanied her arrival. Nathan checked his hair with his hand as she came closer. Aaron just stood patiently and gulped. Benjamin stared at his feet.

"First timers?" she asked, spinning a lanyard around her finger.

"Uh huh," Nathan manage to say.

"Didn't they tell you not to go near the water until your swim test?"

"No." Nathan's face turned pink and then red.

The older girl cocked her head and looked from one boy to another. She grinned.

"You three gonna give me trouble this session?"

"No, ma-am," said Nathan.

"Uh uh," said Aaron.

Benjamin shook his head.

"Well good. I'm Isabelle the head lifeguard. What are your names?"

Each boy mumbled their name.

"Good to meet you and welcome to camp. Now why don't you all head up to the chow hall. The opening ceremony starts in fifteen minutes. You won't wanna miss it."

Without another word, Isabelle turned and walked back toward the lifeguard tower. Nathan whistled softly.

"Wow..." he said.

The other boys just bobbed their heads.

* * *

Camp Wahamalican's director was an older man name Mr. Hendrix. He reminded Benjamin a little bit of Old Kennedy. Mr. Hendrix had long white hair that he tied in a ponytail. He was wiry trim and wore khaki shorts. Benjamin could tell he was a nice man by the way he smiled and joked with the campers. It was funny that adults thought that kids couldn't tell whether a grown-up was nice or not. Benjamin could always tell by a smile (real or fake, nice or not) or their eyes (kind or mean, happy or angry).

Mr. Hendrix told the campers about Camp Wahamalican's history and how it had once been an Indian burial site.

"And sometimes the ancient Indian elders come out at night to say hello," Mr. Hendrix said. There was silence in the large room. "But don't worry, we've made sure only the nice ones stuck around."

There were nervous chuckles and a couple whimpers from new campers. Benjamin wasn't worried about ghosts.

After telling them about the camp rules and eating schedule, the campers were released to their tribes. Tribe Tomahawk's chief was a tall skinny red haired boy named Tony. He said they could call him Tomahawk Tony. The younger boys laughed. Tomahawk Tony gave his own set of rules (no talking after midnight, no sneaking food into the cabin, etc..) as they walked back to the Tomahawk cabin. There were a total of twelve Tomahawk campers. Since it was a tribe for twelve-year-olds, Benjamin was the youngest.

When they arrived back at the cabin, Tony asked Benjamin to stay outside. He waited until the other boys spilled in to speak.

"Benjamin, I'm not sure how you got assigned to this cabin..." Benjamin eyes widened a bit. He didn't want to be sent to another tribe. "...but Mr. Hendrix said you've skipped a couple grades. I just wanted to make sure you're going to be okay with the older guys."

"I came with two of my friends, Nathan and Aaron."

"Nathan's the tall kid, right?"

Benjamin nodded.

"Okay. But you make sure you come tell me if anyone picks on you. I don't put up with bullying in my tribe," said Tony, seriously. Benjamin breathed a sigh of relief.

"Okay."

"Good, now why don't you go get changed for your swim test."

CHAPTER 18

MYSTERY

Benjamin, Nathan and Aaron breezed through the swim test. Aaron had been on swim teams since he was seven. He'd already been picked out by one of the counselors that coached the camp swim competition.

All of the Tomahawks passed the highest level of swimming. That meant they could do any of the water activities and use the water playground. They all hooted and hollered as they split into teams and played a game called 'walk the plank.'

Nathan, being the strongest and one of the fastest of the Tomahawks, ended up winning. Benjamin was one of the first to be thrown off. He didn't care. It was still fun and none of the boys treated him like a baby. That's what he'd wanted. It probably helped that the other Tomahawks already knew that he was best friends with Nathan. Benjamin was glad about the decision to invite his friend along.

After swimming they hiked back to their cabin and grabbed clothes to take showers. They cleaned up quickly and followed Tony to the chow hall.

Their first real meal at Camp Wahamalican felt like a feast. Everyone was hungry after the excitement of the day. Benjamin ate two hamburgers and a huge pile of fries. Nathan ate three hamburgers and saved room for three helpings of dessert.

Full and happy the campers were ushered to their first camp fire. There would be one every week with the final fire coming the night before they all went home. Tonight the camp counselors would perform skits and tell ghost stories.

The entire event went off without a hitch. They were all laughing and retelling the best jokes as they walked back to the cabin. Benjamin stifled a yawn when he noticed a flickering light in the distance. He asked Tony about it.

"Oh that's some old guy that's lived up in the hills for years. Lots of stories about him. Make sure you stay away from his place. I heard about a kid that got chased out with a shotgun..."

Benjamin wasn't listening. Instead he was staring at the flickering flame on the hillside. For some reason it felt like it was calling to him.

That night the nightmares came back. Benjamin tossed and turned in the unfamiliar bunk. At one point he caught himself just as he was going to roll off the bed and onto the floor. Somehow he didn't wake anyone. None of the dreams stuck. He couldn't remember what they were about. The dreams merely left him with a feeling that he was falling... or was it flying?

CHAPTER 19

CAMP STUFF

The first full day of camp was filled with activity. Benjamin enjoyed all his morning classes, but was ready to see his friends at lunch. The other older kids that weren't in Tomahawk looked at him funny all morning.

Nathan couldn't stop talking as they ate peanut butter and jelly sandwiches with a layer of crispy crunchy potato chips in between. It was a habit Benjamin had recently picked up from Nathan.

"I wish you guys were in my archery class," said Nathan. "It was awesome. The counselor said I have a natural gift." Benjamin's ears perked up at the sound of the word 'gift'. "Can you believe it? I've never even picked up a bow before!"

And so it went for the rest of lunch. Benjamin told his friends about what he'd learned in craftsmanship and Aaron instructed them in the proper way to hogtie a prisoner. The counselor teaching his wilderness survival class was a tough old Marine who liked to demonstrate his knot tying techniques on campers. It was all in good fun, of course.

Lunch was done and the three companions split up for their afternoon sessions.

Benjamin was headed to the lake for his first canoeing lesson when someone called his name.

"Benjamin!"

He looked around, not picking out the voice until the other campers cleared. Benjamin's eyes widened. It was Emily, the girl he'd saved.

"Benjamin!" her smile was wide as she made her way over. Benjamin marveled as her ponytail swung and bounced as she walked.

"Hey!"

"Hi."

"I didn't know you were coming."

"Yeah."

She waited for him to say something else. Instead he kicked a rock and avoided her gaze.

"Are you okay?" asked Emily.

Benjamin didn't know how to reply. Whenever he saw her in the halls at school he'd had a whole period to think about and muster the courage just to say, "Hi."

"I'm okay. When…uh, where are you going?"

"Oh! I'm going to canoeing. You?"

He blushed. "Uh, me too."

"Great! Can I walk with you?"

He nodded and they went on their way. As they walked she talked and Benjamin tried not to say anything stupid or trip over his feet.

This was Emily's second summer at camp. She liked the classes he'd chosen. She'd taken most of them the summer before. Canoeing was the only class they had together. It made Benjamin a little sad.

Emily hadn't come with anyone. She did have a lot of friends from the summer before. Some of them waved to her as they neared the lake.

"Have you ever canoed before?" she asked.

"Just a couple times with my dad," croaked Benjamin. He couldn't seem to make his mouth work the way he wanted.

"I tried it last summer during free time. I think it's gonna be a really fun class."

"Yeah," he managed to get out.

Emily was right. Canoeing turned out to be a lot of fun. The teacher, a slightly chubby teenager named Rankin, was really funny and made the nervous campers laugh. He was also very serious about safety and made sure each camper could recite the rules before they were allowed into a canoe.

Despite his size, Benjamin took to canoeing like a bird to flight. By the end of the hour he'd manned the back of one of the canoes and was easily maneuvering in and around the floating buoys. Even Rankin noticed.

"It's Benjamin, right?"

Benjamin nodded.

"I wasn't too sure about you, kid, but I think you're a natural. Good job."

Benjamin thanked the counselor and silently enjoyed the pat on the back. It wasn't often that he was singled out for doing something good when it came to physical fitness.

Emily said goodbye and promised to find him at free time later that night. Benjamin stowed his life jacket and walked down a new trail to his next class: Wilderness Discovery.

The instructor for Wilderness Discovery was a very fat man named Jeremy. He told the campers that he'd been a counselor for twelve years. Benjamin wondered how the man could be so large if he spent his summers outdoors. Maybe it was all the good desserts in the chow hall.

"Today we'll be taking a little hike. I want you all to stay quiet and just keep your eyes and ears open. Soak up the forest. Let it speak to you. I'll point out a few things as we go."

Some of the other campers rolled their eyes and snickered.

"Shhh," said Jeremy, his eyes twinkling with excitement. It looked like he was really into the discovery part of wilderness. He looked out of place for what he did for a living.

For the next forty minutes they followed the counselor down the meandering path. Birds sang and chipmunks scurried away through underbrush as the campers passed. Just as they were going to turn around and head back, Benjamin glimpsed something in the distance. He squinted and shaded his eyes from the sun with his hands. It was a cabin on a hill. A shiver ran down Benjamin's back. Was that the old hermit's place?

Before he could investigate further, Jeremy announced, "Back the way we came, campers."

He scooted past Benjamin, panting a bit from the exertion with rosy cheeks. None of the campers seemed out of breath.

Benjamin took one last look at the cabin and followed the others.

———

After dinner the campers were allowed to have free time when they could roam around camp, swim in the lake, buy things from the camp store or just hang out.

Emily found Benjamin and his friends in the camp store that smelled like leather and peppermint. He introduced her to Nathan and Aaron.

"We were in Mrs. Tabberson's first grade class together, right?" asked Nathan.

"Uh huh," answered Emily.

Benjamin paid for his candy and soda. Emily picked out a bag of Jolly Ranchers and a Gatorade.

They all left the bustling shop and looked for a place to sit. Dusk was falling and campers lounged everywhere. Benjamin dodged a Frisbee as they walked.

"Sorry," an older boy said.

Benjamin waved back.

Nathan pointed to a short stone wall up ahead.

"Dibs on the end," he said.

They all sat down and dug into their goodies. It felt like real freedom to all of them. For Benjamin and Nathan, it was their first time away from home without a family member. Instead of being homesick, they were excited and giddy. They chatted about their favorite parts of the day while stuffing their mouths full of sweets and treats.

At one point Nathan laughed so hard that soda came out of his nose. It was almost contagious as the others snorted along with him.

"All campers have ten minutes to report back to their cabins for night prep," came the voice over the camp-wide speaker system.

Everyone around them responded with a moan. Benjamin didn't mind. He was tired from the day and the lack of sleep the night before.

"See you tomorrow," said Emily. The three Tomahawks waved to her and headed the opposite direction.

CHAPTER 20

THE CALL

Benjamin had just fallen asleep when he woke with a start. His fellow tribe members had been asleep for over an hour. What woke him and no one else? He sat listening. Suddenly there was a outside. It was faint. It sounded like a baby crying. What was a baby doing at camp?

Benjamin laid his head back down and tried to fall back to sleep. The sound came again, "Waaaa…" It sounded louder this time. Why wasn't anyone doing anything about the baby? He plugged his ears with his fingers and closed his eyes tight. "Waaa…" It was even louder!

Looking around the room, Benjamin was amazed that no one else heard the noise. He swung his legs off the bed and silently crept over to the screen door. Tomahawk Tony was snoring loudly on the bunk closest to the exit.

Benjamin peered out into the darkness.

"Waaa…"

He almost jumped at the sound. Steadying himself against the door he tried to pinpoint where the sound was coming from.

"Waaa…"

Benjamin was almost positive that the noise came from the woods. He cocked his ear.

"Waaa…"

He was right. It wasn't coming from the permanently lit area around the chow hall and staff building.

"Waaa…"

The crying seemed to become more and more urgent.

Benjamin walked over to where Tony was sleeping. He bent down and nudged the counselor. Tony kept snoring. Benjamin shook Tony's shoulder. Still nothing. Finally he whispered, "Tony." Tony didn't move.

Next Benjamin snuck back to his bunk, stepped up on the ledge and tried to wake Nathan. The same thing happened. He wouldn't wake up.

"Waaa…" came the incessant call.

Why wasn't any of the camp staff doing anything and why wasn't anyone else waking up?

Taking a deep breath to calm himself, Benjamin slipped on his shoes and grabbed a flashlight. He normally wasn't so brave. Something about being at camp away from the real world emboldened him, or was it the fact that he had a 'gift'?

Benjamin tried to rouse Tony one last time. Nothing. Weird.

Glancing back one last time, Benjamin clicked on his flashlight, opened the screen door, and stepped out into the darkness.

"Waaaaaaa! Waaaaa!"

It was easy for Benjamin to follow the crying. Not only did it come at regular intervals, it also seemed to be getting louder. He crept slowly, shining his tiny flashlight all around. At some point he picked up a sturdy stick that could be used as a weapon if needed. Benjamin didn't know how effective it might be with his hands trembling.

"Waaaaa!"

His little flashlight didn't cut that far into the night. Unfortunately the clouds covered the full moon as he walked farther and farther into the woods. Dodging branches and logs Benjamin did his best to maintain a straight course. He lost all track of time and realized he didn't have his watch on.

"Waaaaa!"

Just as he stepped around a large oak tree, using his hand to guide himself around, the clouds parted revealing the moon. The moon's light shown down and what Benjamin saw made him inhale sharply.

Now illuminated by the celestial night were two forms, some kind of animal (it was what was making the horrible crying sound) and a huge man. Benjamin could only see the man's back. He seemed to be doing something to the animal. With the added light Benjamin could see that it was a baby deer.

"Are ya just gonna sit there, or are ya gonna come help me hold this poor thing down?" the large man called.

Benjamin looked all around. Who was the man talking to? He couldn't be talking to Benjamin.

"Well?" the man asked turning. He looked straight at Benjamin. Lit by the moon the man's features looked spooky.

He wore an unruly thick beard that complimented his shaggy hair.

"Come give me a hand will ya?"

For some reason Benjamin didn't run. Maybe it was because the man, although he looked wild, didn't actually appear threatening. Maybe it was because Benjamin was curious. Most surprisingly, the boy found that he was no longer scared.

He marched over to the man and said, "How can I help?"

Benjamin could now see that the man was fiddling with the deer's leg. There was something attached to it and the leg was covered in blood that looked black in the night.

"Help me hold it down. It keeps kicking and I can't get this darned trap off."

Benjamin liked animals, but he'd never touched a wild animal, unless you counted the fish and crawdads he'd caught the summer before with his dad. Avoiding the fawn's head, he placed his hands gently against its torso.

The scraggly giant mumbled to himself as he worked, "Darned cuts…stupid youngsters…have to talk to the director…" The murmering and the fiddling continued for a couple minutes until finally the man exclaimed, "Got it!" With a yank he pulled the remaining cord away. His hand was bloody. He didn't seem to care.

"Okay. On the count of three I want you to let go and jump back. I don't want this thing to buck you. It's young but they still have hard heads and hooves."

Benjamin nodded.

"One, two, three!"

Benjamin let go of the animal and it sprang up. Without any sign of a limp the deer bolted out of sight.

"Will it be okay with the cut on its leg?" asked Benjamin, his eyes wide with wonder.

Standing the man took out a rag and wiped the blood from his massive hands. "She'll be fine. How about I thank you with a nice warm cup of hot chocolate."

Normally Benjamin never would have said yes to such a request. The man was a stranger and possibly dangerous. His mom would freak if she knew he was out in the woods alone, talking to a bearded giant that looked like he lived in the hills.

"I…I'm not sure I should."

"I understand. After all, you'd be crazy to listen to a mountain man like me, right, Benjamin?"

Benjamin froze at the sound of his name. He slowly backed away putting one foot behind the other.

"Now hold on. I didn't mean to scare you, Benjamin."

Benjamin moved faster at hearing his name a second time. Who was this hulking man?

"Kennedy told me you were coming."

Benjamin stopped. Had he heard right?

"What?"

"I said Kennedy told me you were coming."

"That's impossible. How did he know?"

The man chuckled deeply. "How do you think your parents found out about camp? We know how to get what we want, Benjamin."

He'd said it matter-of-factly like you might say "I'm going to the bathroom," but to Benjamin the thought of someone else manipulating his life raised goosebumps all over his body. Who were these people?

"Now don't worry your little head. I ain't gonna hurt you. We just thought it'd be best to have someone nearby to keep an eye on you."

"Why do you need to keep an eye on me?"

The man's grin faded for a moment then reappeared.

"I…uh…I mean we know how hard it is when you first get your gift. It's important to have someone close by just in case, you know?"

Benjamin didn't look convinced. Maybe it was the man's hesitation that had him feeling suspicious.

"What about Kennedy?"

"What about him?"

"I thought he was my teacher."

"Well, he is, but seeing as how I live the closest…"

"Are you going to teach me?" asked Benjamin, his eyes glittering in the moonlight.

"Err, no. I'm not a destructor like you and Kennedy. I'm a…"

"You're a healer!"

"You picked that up did you?"

Benjamin nodded. "I saw the deer's leg. It was all cut up. You helped it didn't you?"

"I did. It's what I do. This one got caught in some new poacher's trap. Haven't seen this kind in these parts before. Reminds me, I need to tell Mr. Hendrix to let his campers know. Don't want any young kids getting snared."

"You know Mr. Hendrix, the camp's director?"

"Sure, sure. Me and Mr. Hendrix go back a long ways. I remember when he only a counselor. We share a pot of tea every now and again. So how about that hot chocolate?"

"But, you haven't told me your name yet," said Benjamin.

"I haven't? Where has my mind gone?" He bowed at the waist. "Wally Goodfriend at your service."

Benjamin giggled. He couldn't help it. He'd assumed the giant man had a tough name like Crusher, Bansif or Maximus.

"Goodfriend? Is that your real last name?"

"It is," Wally smiled. "Passed down through my daddy's side of the family. Used to be Godfreid when they first moved to America. Changed it to Goodfriend when my great grand-dad opened a bakery in New Orleans: Goodfriend's Goodies. I can still smell the caramel rolls."

Wally closed his eyes and sniffed the air. Benjamin giggled again. The tall man looked silly sniffing the air like a happy puppy.

CHAPTER 21

HOT COCOA AND COMPANY

It turned out that Wally owned the log cabin where Benjamin had seen the flickering light coming from on the walk the day before. Outside it looked a little rundown. Inside was anything but. Cozy oversized leather chairs (a must if you were as big as Wally Goodfriend) sat in front of a large stone fireplace. It smelled homey with a mix of herbs and chocolate. In the corner was a modern flat panel television currently showing a muted episode of some National Geographic special. The rest of the one story cabin was filled with a large dining room table made out of the trunk of some huge tree. By the number of rings in it Benjamin knew it had been a very old tree.

All along the walls were pictures of Wally throughout the years. Most were taken outdoors with animals. There was one of Wally with tow shaggy horses that bore a striking resemblance to the big man.

Wally told Benjamin that he'd chosen a personal path of helping animals. He loved them and they in turn loved him. Wally said there was even a family of black bears that came to the cabin before hibernating to get bit of his famous blackberry pie. Benjamin shivered at the thought. He couldn't imagine coming face to face with a bear.

They settled for the first, then a second cup of creamy hot chocolate. Benjamin had never had anything like it. It was like drinking a milky chocolate bar. Delicious.

"So how did you end up here, Wally?" asked Benjamin, wiping away another hot chocolate mustache with a soiled cloth napkin.

The huge man took a large swig of his drink (his mug was three times the size of Benjamin's) and wiped his mouth with the back of his hand.

"I barely remember. Some years ago, I was travelling the country on foot working odd jobs as I went. A lot of farmers took me on for my size. I could bail hay like nobody's business. Pretty soon they'd find out that I was good with the animals. Saved quite a few cows, goats and even a couple horses. More than one farmer asked that I stay on full time. It'd save them the money of having to go to the vet. Anyway, I wandered for a couple years and made it up here probably twenty years ago. Built this place with my own two hands."

"How do you make money?"

"All kinds of ways. I've bred animals, sometimes I do some work for the camp with the horses. But mostly I make money on the internet."

Benjamin almost spit out his drink.

"What?" he blurted.

"You'd be amazed at what you can find out in the woods, antlers, pelts, all from animals that are already dead, of course, even found some gold once in one of the rivers a couple miles away. That kept me fed for almost a year! I'm pretty handy with carving too. Have a small shop in the back where I do all my woodwork. I get some great pieces of wood and make all kinds of things out of 'em. Have one gentleman that's bought almost twenty of my duck carvings. He's a collector."

Benjamin stared at Wally with wide eyes. Working on a farm he could believe, but making a living on the internet seemed impossible.

Wally made to pour some more hot cocoa for them both, but Benjamin waved him away as he yawned.

"I should probably go."

The big man looked up at the wood clock.

"Oops! I better walk you down there. No tellin' what's out right now. Don't want you getting' lost either."

The way Wally went it only took fifteen minutes to get back to the camp. They parted ways at the edge of the woods overlooking Benjamin's cabin.

"You may want to keep this outing to yourself, Benjamin. I wouldn't want you getting into any trouble."

"Don't worry, I won't."

He stuck out his hand and Wally enveloped it with his.

"It was a great meeting you, Wally."

"And you too, Benjamin. Have a good night."

Wally turned and disappeared in the night.

All of Benjamin's creeping into the cabin was wasted because everyone was still fast asleep. He crawled into bed and looked up at the wooden slats above. Benjamin was happier than he'd ever been.

That night he slept better than he had in a long, long time.

CHAPTER 22

THE MOHAWKS

The next morning Benjamin was the first to get up and dressed. He was ready for the day. For some reason, instead of being tired from the events of the night before, he was energized and clear-headed.

Nathan stifled a yawn as he put on his camp t-shirt. They weren't mandatory, but Nathan liked them more than the shirts he'd brought from home.

Aaron walked over picking a piece of sleep out from the corner of his eye.

"I wonder what's for breakfast," said Nathan.

They left the cabin to find out.

———

Benjamin could see dark clouds on the horizon as they walked to the chow hall. He wondered what camp was like during a rainstorm. Maybe they'd have indoor games. He hadn't seen a television yet so he doubted there'd be a movie day like they had at school sometimes.

The boys smelled the bacon as they approached the squat one-story building where they ate.

"I'm gonna eat a whole plate of just bacon," announced Nathan.

Benjamin and Aaron laughed.

———

After getting their fills of pancakes and bacon Benjamin excused himself to go find Emily. He'd seen her from across the large dining hall. Nathan and Aaron exchanged knowing glances, but didn't say anything. Benjamin didn't notice the looks.

Maneuvering through the throngs of campers either still eating or getting up to clear their plates, Benjamin caught Emily's eye and waved. She smiled back. Benjamin's stomach flipped. He gulped as he drifted closer, trying to look nonchalant.

"Hey, Emily," said Benjamin, as he sidled up to her table. The other girls huffed and looked away. Emily rolled her eyes and gave another grand smile to Benjamin.

"Did you hear about the storm?" she asked.

"No. I saw the clouds coming though," he replied as he scooted in next to her on the bench.

"That'll mean no water sports today. I was really looking forward to being out on the lake."

"So what do we do instead?"

Emily shrugged. "Depending on how bad the storm is they'll probably make us stay inside somewhere. I heard that one time the campers and staff all had to sleep in the staff building when tornados came through."

Benjamin's didn't like the sound of that, unless he got to hang out with Emily. "Tornados?"

"Yeah. One of the counselors told us about…"

Just then they heard the siren from one of the camp speakers. That meant an announcement was coming.

"Attention counselors and staff. Due to an incoming severe thunderstorm all outdoor activities will be cancelled for today. A new schedule will be given to tribe leaders within the hous. Until then please make your way back to your cabins. Thank you."

"I guess we better get going," said Emily. She almost looked sad.

"Okay. See you later?"

She nodded and got up to join her friends.

Benjamin quickly made his way back to Nathan and Aaron. Nathan was hurriedly shoveling one last handful of bacon into his mouth. They grabbed their trays and deposited them in the waste area along with everyone else.

By the time they got outside, the sky was completely overcast. They could smell the rain and the air felt heavy.

"This is gonna be a big storm," Aaron guessed as he gazed up at the rolling clouds.

Meandering down the cabin path they passed a group of older boys huddled together. Just as Benjamin and his friends walked by, the boys dispersed and discretely surrounded

Benjamin. It was Nathan who noticed the move first. He shifted closer to Benjamin.

"Hey, shortcake," said one of the boys. Benjamin ignored the comment. Unable to let the comment pass, Nathan turned his head.

"Who are you talking to?" he asked the other group. There were five of them, all wearing camp t-shirts with 'Mohawk Tribe' written in black permanent marker on their sleeves. They'd heard about the already infamous Mohawk Tribe. Apparently they were one more infraction away from getting split up or maybe even kicked out of camp. You never knew with the rumors that passed from camper to camper like an out of control virus.

"I'm talking to your tiny friend there."

"Yeah," said another boy, this one had blond hair hanging down to his cheek. He kept flipping it back and to the side to keep it out of his eyes. "We need a new mascot and heard yours might be available."

The rest of the Mohawk boys snickered at the comment. Nathan stopped dead in his tracks. Benjamin sighed. He hated bullies, but he didn't want his friends getting in trouble because of him.

"It's okay, Nathan. Just ignore…"

Nathan held his hand up motioned for Benjamin to be quiet and stay back. His face had turned from a light pink to a darker red.

"Looks like big boy's getting mad," said the blonde kid. Nathan was larger than any of the older boys. Apparently, they thought their numbers would intimidate their foes.

"You shut your mouth or I'll shut it for you," growled Nathan, clenching his fists until his knuckles turned white.

"Oooo!" said the Mohawks in unison.

"What going on over here?" came an adult voice. It was Mr. Hendrix, the camp director. The gathering crowd had alerted him to the problem.

"Uh, nothing, Mr. Hendrix," said the blond antagonist, not quite convincingly.

The usually genial face of Mr. Hendrix glared at the Mohawk boys.

"Are they bothering you, Mr. Dragon?"

Benjamin hated it when he got singled out by adults. He thought that maybe it was because he was the shortest and most likely to be on the receiving end of bullying.

"Uh, no, sir. We were just talking."

Mr. Hendrix could smell the lie. He didn't say anything though. From his years working at Camp Wahamalican, he knew it wasn't unusual to have small cliques form amongst the campers. He did not tolerate bullies, however. He'd been known to send campers home without a warning if the offense warranted it. Camp Wahamalican had a strict no bullying policy.

After another moment of innocent eyes from the Mohawk boys, seething by Nathan, feet staring by Benjamin, Mr. Hendrix finally said, "You boys better get back to your cabins. I don't want you to get caught in the rain."

The Mohawks were the first to leave. Nathan was still breathing hard when Mr. Hendrix put a calming hand on his shoulder. "It's okay, son. Why don't you get on back now."

There was sadness in Nathan's eyes. He knew that just a few month's before, he'd been just like the Mohawk boys, a bully trying to look cool. It made him angry and upset at the same time.

"Yes, sir," Nathan replied with sagging shoulders.

Benjamin, Nathan and Aaron walked in silence as they made their way back to Tomahawk Cabin.

CHAPTER 23

THE STORM

Thirty minutes later, the promised announcement came over the loudspeaker. The campers were given the choice of either going to the chow hall to play games or stay in their cabins until the storm blew over.

As much as Benjamin wanted to see Emily, he was no longer in the mood. He didn't want to risk the chance of running into the Mohawks again. Instead he, Nathan, Aaron and two of the other Tomahawk boys elected to stay put and play cards.

"Make sure you don't go wandering off, okay?" said Tomahawk Tony as he left. All the boys nodded and turned their attention back to the game. Nathan was teaching them a new game he'd learned from one of the guys that worked at his dad's auto body shop.

Minutes later, they paused as the rain started as a light pitter pat and quickly became a thumping downpour. They shut the windows and door so the blowing rain wouldn't come in. After listening to the rain and thunder for a minute, they diverted their attention back to the game. They already had flashlights standing by in case the power went out.

Benjamin picked up the gist of the game faster than even Nathan who was the only one who'd played before. They played round after round, only stopping once to eat the bagged lunches Tomahawk Tony brought wrapped in a large plastic bag.

Before they knew it, dusk had fallen. The current tally was fifteen games for Benjamin, five for Nathan, four for Aaron, and two each for the other Tomahawks when someone knocked on the door.

"Did you lock it?" Nathan asked the boy sitting next to him.

"Nope. I'll go see who it is."

He hopped up and walked to the door. When he opened it they saw a skinny pimple faced boy standing and shivering.

"You need to help me," he said.

The skinny boy was from the Sioux Tribe. Their cabin was two down from Tomahawks. He'd already been to two other cabins, but everyone had left for the chow hall. In between rapid breaths, sounding like he had asthma, the boy told them that some Mohawks had raided their cabin and taken one of the other Sioux campers. They said they were going to tie him up in the woods and leave him. The Sioux Tribe Leader was at the dining hall so the boy thought finding other campers would be faster.

"You have to help!" the boy pleaded.

The Tomahawks all looked at each other. Nathan punched a fist into his palm.

"I'll help," he said.

"I'll come too," said Benjamin. Everyone looked at him in surprise. He ignored their stares.

"I can go get the counselors," said Aaron.

A plan was quickly decided. The skinny Sioux kid, Aaron and the others would go to the dining hall. Nathan and Benjamin would go after the Mohawks.

The Sioux camper pointed in the direction the Mohawks had gone. Nathan took off at a sprint. Benjamin wasn't far behind.

———

They plodded on through the drenching rain. The constant flashes of lightning lit the way. Benjamin's flashlight glowed pathetically in comparison.

"I think I see something up there," said Nathan, pointing ahead.

Slowing their pace, Benjamin wiped rain off of his face and tried to see what Nathan was talking about. A flickering light strobed in the distance.

"You think that's them?" asked Benjamin.

"Who else would it be?"

A muted scream sounded in the direction of the blinking lights.

"Come on. Let's go."

Dodging creepy grabbers and whipping branches, they huffed their way closer, the lights increasing as the distance closed. The view cleared and they saw it.

A hundred feet away a small boy was tied to a tree with some kind of cloth gag around his mouth. His eyes bulged in fright.

The Mohawk boys were dancing around the tree like Indians. Each held a flashlight as they shouted gibberish that sounded vaguely like an ancient Indian dialect. One kid even wore a feather, now soaked to a single line, under a bandana wrapped around his head.

"Leave him alone!" screamed Nathan over the thundering wind.

The Mohawks stopped their dancing and looked up fearfully. They thought a camp counselor had found them. They pointed their flashlights at the newcomers and the tension in their faces calmed when they saw who it was. It was the blonde boy from earlier who spoke first.

"Looky, looky. Husky and the dwarf decided to come visit."

There were laughs all around. It sounded funny in the heavy rain like a babbling brook running over well-worn river rocks.

"I said let him go," repeated Nathan.

"Are you gonna make me?"

The Mohawks all stepped closer to Nathan and Benjamin. One boy stood quietly, eyes glaring. Another kept grabbing his glasses and wiping them with his soppy wet t-shirt. A third stayed back, looking unsure. The last boy looked on with an amused grin like a cat watching a stupid mouse.

The blonde Mohawk tried to shove Nathan, but he'd underestimated his adversary's skill. Nathan grabbed the boy's left upper arm, turned to the right, and threw the Mohawk onto the muddy ground.

Struggling to get up from his sloppy face plant, the Mohawk yelled to his friends, "Get him!"

The smug boy closest to his target charged first. He met the same fate as his buddy and actually served to knock the blonde over like a bowling ball taking out a pin. The rest of the small group hesitated as Benjamin joined his friend. He wasn't a coward.

"Who's next?" snarled Nathan.

Before anyone could answer, a pinkish-orange haze illuminated the area, followed by a thunderous *BOOM*. Lightning struck the ancient tree the Sioux boy was fixed to and the horrifying *CRAAAACK* sounded like a giant snapping the tree in two.

The prisoner screamed and fainted just as the tree fell forward.

The other boys scattered and ran away shrieking like scared little girls. Nathan and Benjamin would be crushed. There was no way around it. Nathan dove to the ground. Benjamin stood fixated on the falling trunk. He stared as if in a trance. In his mind, his thoughts were clear. *Stop the tree.*

As if on cue, the tree's descent halted. Benjamin cocked his head as if admiring something curious in a toy shop window. He blinked. Still the rain pounded down. The tree did not. It hung in the air like the spoon Old Kennedy had shown him in the ice cream shop.

"Dragon?" came the awestruck voice from Nathan.

Benjamin ignored his friend. He didn't want to get distracted. This was the first time he'd actually controlled his 'gift'.

Marveling at the clarity, Benjamin slowly spun and then eased the massive tree down onto its side so the trapped boy wouldn't get crushed. Nathan rushed over to the unconscious boy. Benjamin stayed put with a big grin on his face. He'd done it. He wasn't crazy. Old Kennedy was right. He did have a gift.

CHAPTER 24

HERO

The Sioux boy woke up halfway back to camp. Except for being half scared to death, he was fine. He thanked Benjamin and Nathan and asked that they not tell anyone about what happened. The last thing he wanted was to be bullied more by the Mohawk boys.

Benjamin knew how he felt. He'd been through it before. Sometimes when you told on a bully (or even worse, your parents did), the harassment got worse. They would keep the secret.

They looked like drowned rats when they got back to their cabin. Everyone was gone.

"I guess we better go tell them it was a false alarm," Nathan suggested.

"Do you mind going alone? I'm gonna get changed."

"But…" Instead of finishing, Nathan looked at his friend and nodded. "I'll bring you some food back, if there's any left."

"Okay."

Nathan walked back out into the driving rain. Benjamin waited two minutes then left through the cabin door. He had to talk to Wally.

He somehow found his way in the dark. Benjamin knocked on the door. There was loud movement from inside. Latches scraped and the door opened flooding firelight through the entryway.

Wally looked down in surprise at the soaked and shivering young man.

"Benjamin? Are you okay?"

Unable to find the words Benjamin just smiled wide, tears of joy mixing with the rain running off his hair. Wally's look turned from worry to confusion when he noticed Benjamin's grinning expression.

"Come in here, you crazy boy."

Benjamin stepped into the welcome warmth of the cozy cabin. He stood on the doormat as Wally went to fetch a towel.

Now sitting comfortably in front of the blazing fire, sipping on a welcome mug of Wally's hot cocoa, Benjamin relayed the story of the falling tree. He explained it matter-of-factly as if he'd just been a bystander instead of the one in the thick of it.

Wally whistled over his steaming mug. "Sounds like you've gotten a bit of a knack for it."

"I'm don't think so. Out there I could do it, but just a second ago I tried to move that log by the fireplace and nothing happened."

Wally chuckled as if remembering a private joke. He stared into the fire contendtedly.

"What?" asked Benjamin.

Wally almost dropped his mug in surprise. "What? Oh, sorry. I was just remembering back to when I first found out about my healing gift. Felt a lot like you do right now. Scared, excited, confused. Sound familiar?"

Benjamin nodded, eager to hear the story.

"Well, we all tend to get our talents around the age of ten."

"When did you find out?"

"I lived on a farm with my parents and my little brother. On the morning of my tenth birthday, my dad woke me up before the sun came up. He told me to keep quiet. I snuck out of the house with him and followed him out to the barn. Waiting for me was the most beautiful chestnut mare I'd ever seen. My dad said it was my first birthday present as a man. You see, by that time I was already taller than most kids in high school. Plus, on the farm everyone chipped in. By the time you turned ten you were considered a man. My dad even let me drive his old pickup around to do errands on the farm.

"Anyway, I gave my dad a big hug and he helped me saddle her up. I remember him telling me that I couldn't name her until I'd ridden her, that way I'd know her spirit and give her a proper naming. The sun was just coming over the horizon as we pranced out of the barn and into the daylight. I'd ridden plenty of horses before so I knew what I was doing. I took my time at first, not wanted to get her tripped up on paths she didn't know yet. It didn't take us long to fall into a

rhythm. We walked, then trotted, then cantered and then gal-
loped at full speed. I was in love. I whispered her name into
her ear and she whinnied: Daylight.

"After a good run around, I pointed her back toward the
house. I was getting hungry and wanted to get her all cleaned
up before I had to start my chores. We were walking along a
little creek that ran the border of our farm. All of a sudden,
Daylight reared back on her hind legs. There was a rattlesnake
in the middle of the path soaking in the sunlight. It was early
for rattlers or I would've been more careful. Well, Daylight
spooked and threw me off. I landed hard and watched, like
it was in slow motion, as she reared back again and one of
her back hooves stepped into a hole. I barely rolled out of the
way or she would've landed right on top of me. Instead she
flopped into the creek with a crash.

"When Daylight fell back, I could heard a loud pop. She
snapped her leg bone clean in two. Now I don't know if you
know this, but most times when that happens to a horse you
have to put them down. Do you know what that means?"

Benjamin nodded. It meant that someone had to kill the
animal so it wouldn't be in really, really bad pain.

"I knew what it meant as soon as I heard the break. My
heart almost burst as she started screaming from the pain.
Staggering to the creek, I watched her thrash and cry. Her leg
was bent backward. I could see the jagged bone coming out.
That's when it happened."

Wally stared into the fire, willing the memory to come.
He smiled at the thought.

"My heart swelled and I could've sworn that I felt what I
can only describe as a warm breeze blow off of me and toward
Daylight. What I saw next I'd only heard about in church on

Sundays. Her screaming stopped and a peaceful look came to her eyes. I thought she'd died. Hot tears ran down my face. Then I noticed she was still breathing. I looked back at her broken leg and watched as it adjusted into how it'd been before the fall. The wound mended together as I stood there. It was like I'd willed it to happen."

Wally sipped his drink.

"What happened next?" prodded Benjamin, his eyes sparkling in amazement.

"Well, Daylight got up and walked over to me. She nuzzled into my chest. I didn't know it then, but animals have this sixth sense about healing. They know when I've helped them. It's how I can have these mean ol' bears hangin' around.

"What about your parents? Did you tell them?"

"Are you kidding? I was too scared to tell them. I thought my mom would take that beautiful horse away. Didn't want to get in trouble."

"I know the feeling," said Benjamin.

"Yeah. I think you destructors have it worse than us healers. At least my gift can only be used for good. That's why Kennedy tries so hard to find any new destructors before they can hurt anyone. I can't imagine the fright you got when yours first came out. Speakin' of fright, I think it's about time you got back. Should be lights out soon down at the camp. Don't want them sending a search party out for you."

Benjamin groaned. He'd like nothing more than to sit in front of the fire and hear more of Wally's stories. The sturdy cabin felt like home.

Benjamin somehow returned just as the other campers were streaming into the Tomahawk cabin. The only one not smiling was Nathan. He glared at Benjamin when he walked in, once again soaked to the bone.

"Where were you?" hissed Nathan.

Benjamin motioned over to their bunks. He wanted to talk where no one else could hear. The rest of the Tomahawks were probably too engaged in tearing off their water-logged clothing to care, but Benjamin didn't want to take any chances.

"Where did you go? I got everyone calmed down at the chow hall and then I come back and you're gone. You had another five minutes and then I was gonna tell Tony that you were gone."

Benjamin hadn't thought that Nathan would be so concerned.

"I'm sorry. I just went for a walk."

"Out in that?!"

"Shhh."

"Are you crazy? We almost get squashed by a tree and you want to go back out in the rain? What if something had happened?" Nathan was breathing hard as he spoke.

"I already told you I was sorry. What are you, my mom now?" Benjamin smiled.

The smile caught Nathan off-guard. He made to blurt out another angry comment and stopped. A laugh burst out of his mouth. Nathan clamped a hand over his mouth.

"You're right. I was just worried. I know you're like all powerful..."

"Shhh..."

"Right. Sorry. I mean. Nevermind. Let's get ready for bed. I'm pooped."

Benjamin was glad his friend had calmed. He never liked people to be upset, especially if it was his fault. The walk to Wally's probably hadn't been the smartest decision, but at the time he'd wanted to be with his own kind, someone who knew what he was going through. It was all so confusing.

With all the excitement of the night coursing through his body, Benjamin knew he'd never fall asleep. He changed into dry set of boxer briefs and shorts, joined the others to brush their teeth at the door with a canteen of water, then hopped into his bed. Much to his surprise, he fell asleep before the lights were off.

CHAPTER 25

LINGERING THREATS

The next morning, the campers walked outside to see what kind of devastation the storm had left behind. To everyone's relief the sun climbed into a clear blue sky. There were branches and debris all over camp. Other than a couple lifeguard umbrellas getting blown into the lake, the camp came away relatively unscathed.

Campers weren't happy about having to help with the cleanup effort. Kids moaned and groaned as they helped counselors and camp staff haul the fallen branches to the large fire pit. They'd use the wreckage for future camp fires once the wood dried out.

After the cleanup, things went back to normal. All were happy to be back in their chosen activities. For Benjamin the return to reality wasn't as exciting. He'd just save a boy's life and he couldn't talk to anyone about it. It felt like a volcano trying to bubble its way out of his chest. He had a hard time concentrating on what his instructors said and one time completely missed his Wilderness Discovery teacher asking him a question. Laughter from the other campers snapped him from his daydreaming.

At lunch Emily sat with the Tomahawk boys. Benjamin envied the way she could so easily move between her different groups of friends. Everyone seemed to like Emily and knew her by name. He was happy claim her as a friend.

After they ate he strolled with Emily toward their canoeing class. She's become quieter than usual. The conversation almost sounded forced. Benjamin cringed inwardly. His mind swirled with possibilities. The most important being: Was she going to stop being his friend?

Emily took a deep breath and said, "Benjamin?"

"Yeah?"

"I, just wanted…I don't know how to say this." She had her eyes locked on the path avoiding eye contact.

Benjamin's stomach dropped like a rock in a deep pool. It had happened before. He'd made one friend at an old school and then the boy had told him that he couldn't be friends anymore. He'd made up some excuse about not having time because of homework or something. Benjamin knew it was a lie. He'd heard the whispers in the halls. The boy was getting teased for being his friend. That's why he couldn't be Benjamin's friend.

Benjamin took a steadying breath. Before the tree incident he might have looked at things differently. He might have felt like crying. Now he just felt sad.

"It's okay, Emily. I understand."

"Huh?"

"I know that you can't be my friend. It's…"

"Wait. What?" She stopped walking. "What are you talking about, Benjamin?"

"I just…I know that the other kids are probably making fun of you for hanging out with me, and…you don't deserve that. It's okay." He tried to put the most understanding looking face on that he could. It looked more like he had to pee in his pants.

Emily started laughing. Benjamin didn't know what to say. First she was going to stop being his friend and now she was laughing at him? It was more than his fragile heart could take. He started walking away, his head hanging.

Still laughing, Emily grabbed him by the arm. He shook it off angrily.

"Benjamin, wait."

"What do you want?"

"You thought I was going to stop being friends with you?" she said quietly.

Benjamin didn't say anything. He stared at his feet instead.

"I'm sorry. I didn't know," said Emily. "But no, I wasn't going to say that."

Benjamin's head snapped up.

"What?"

"I was going to tell you…I mean I…I wanted to say thank you for…for saving my life."

Benjamin blushed and averted his eyes.

"Well…I didn't really save your life. Err…the car swerved and missed you."

"I know, but I wasn't paying attention and I think the car swerved because you were running toward me."

They stood quietly, each avoiding the other's look. Thankfully Emily changed the subject.

"I guess we should be getting to canoeing, huh?"

Benjamin breathed a sigh of relief.

"Yeah, uh, let's go before they stick us with that fat canoe."

Emily giggled. It was a glorious sound to Benjamin and he soaked it up as they once again went on their way.

The campers in the canoeing class had a splash battle that day. They were given small buckets and the instructor let them use their paddles. In order to win, teams had to keep their canoe upright (using the buckets to throw water could be effective, but only if you didn't tip your canoe in the process) and keep water out of your canoe. Emily told Benjamin that the winner was usually the canoe that didn't flip.

After close to twenty minutes of paddling, splashing, hollering and laughing Benjamin and Emily's canoe was the last one of ten standing, or at least floating upright. Their prize was not having to help clean up the canoes and gear for the rest of the week, and bragging rights, of course.

"That was amazing!" said Emily as they walked away from the lake. They had a thirty minute break until their next classes. "You were awesome steering us around the other canoes."

Benjamin blushed for what felt like the millionth time. Do you ever stop blushing around pretty girls when they compliment you?

"You were the one that kept splashing everyone with the bucket. How did you stay up so easily? Everyone else kept falling or tipping."

Emily shrugged nonchalantly. "Must be the gymnastics my mom made me take when I was little. Hey, wanna go over to the store? I'd kill for a soda right now."

Benjamin agreed. They chatted happily as they walked.

When they arrived at the camp store an unfortunate scene greeted Benjamin. The five Mohawk boys they'd chased into the woods were leaning against the wall outside the store.

Emily saw Benjamin's face tighten.

"What?" she asked.

"I don't feel like going in anymore."

Emily looked up at the store and saw the Mohawk boys.

"Have they been picking on you?"

"No," said Benjamin, not quite convincingly.

"Look. I know the blonde one. He's the ring leader. His name is Manning. He almost got kicked out last year. You can stay out here if you want, but it would be really nice if you could come in with me."

Her pleading look won him over. Benjamin assented. The pair walked up to the store. One of the boys noticed Benjamin and nudged Manning. The five Mohawks stopped talking and watched with narrowed eyes. Benjamin did his best to keep his eyes facing forward.

Inside Emily chose an orange soda and a candy bar. Benjamin opted for a pack of gum, a small bottle of grape juice, and a bag of Doritos. They paid by signing their chits and stepped out into the heat. The Mohawks were waiting.

"Hey, Emily," sneered Manning, tossing his blonde hair back.

"Hi, Manning," said Emily without stopping.

"Why don't you hang out with us? As long as you don't bring your little friend." The other Mohawks laughed.

Emily wheeled around to face the blonde bully.

"I heard they kicked you out of riding again. Was it because you smell worse than the goats? You really should take a shower you know." She smiled innocently and batted her eyes. Manning frowned and the vein on his forehead bulged.

"Never mind. Maybe you should go hang out with your boyfriend and the loser Tomahawks," said Manning.

"He's not my boyfriend."

"Emily and Dragon, sitting in a tree, K-I-S-S-I-N-G…" the rest of Mohawks sang along.

Emily turned around and took off at a fast walk. Benjamin followed.

"This ain't over Dragon!" Manning called over the singing of his gang. Benjamin kept walking.

"I hate him," said Emily once out of sight of the Mohawks.

"How do you know him?"

"He was really nice when we first got to camp last year. Then for some reason he just started being mean. Promise me you'll never do that, Benjamin."

"Of course." Benjamin almost laughed at the thought. Him a bully? Then Old Kennedy's words came back to him. As a destructor could he go bad? He shivered at the thought.

CHAPTER 26

BACK TO NORMAL

The next few days went by in a flash. When Benjamin wasn't in class, he either spent time with his Tomahawk friends, with Emily, or both. Nothing else happed with the Mohawks. It seemed as though they'd learned their lesson.

Benjamin was as happy as he'd ever been. Sure he missed his parents, but that was more like a minor ache in the pit of his stomach. Kind of like the feeling of forgetting something and not really remembering what you forgot.

Some nights he'd sneak out and spend time with Wally. He always had a hundred questions for the gentle giant. One time Wally even let him pet a family of deer he'd helped the year before. They still came back to say hello and see what treats Wally had for them. They loved apples and bananas.

One night Benjamin asked his friend about when he'd be able to control his gift whenever he wanted.

"We all develop differently. It's pretty similar to being an athlete or an artist. The more they practice the better they get. The same goes for us. I've known one or two healers that couldn't do more than fix bumps and bruises. They just didn't have the drive to do more. I didn't understand how they could be happy with that, but they were."

"So what about me?"

"Let me guess. The only times it's worked for you are when you've been in trouble or there was an emergency, right?"

"How did you know?"

"That's how it starts with all of us. First and foremost, our gifts are emotional. We don't wave silly wands or say strange words to cast spells. More than anything, our gifts seem to come from within us. Does that make sense?"

Benjamin's face scrunched as he tried to understand.

"I think so."

"Look, I wouldn't worry about it much. I know it's probably really cool for you when it happens, but until you're older you don't need to be perfect with it. For now I'd say learn to control your emotions. I've heard that most destructors go bad when they go through puberty, or worse, when they go to high school."

"Why's that?"

"You haven't been there yet so you haven't felt it. Pretty soon your emotions will be all over the place, like a bee stuck in a jar. Sometimes you don't know which way is up or down. Throw in girls and dealing with other kids going through the same thing...it's a wonder any of us make it out of our teenage years!"

Benjamin only understood parts of what Wally was saying. He got that his gift worked when some powerful emotion coursed through his body. That would explain the fight with Nathan, the car with Emily, and the tree in the woods.

"How long do I have to wait?" Benjamin asked.

Wally shrugged.

"Like I said, we're all different. Mine developed pretty fast on the farm since I had so many animals to take care of. Now you…it might be hard to go around saving people from falling trees all the time." Wally winked at Benjamin.

Benjamin wished there was some way he could jump-start the process. He wanted to control his gift. It frightened him to think of what might happen if he really hurt someone because he couldn't manage it.

CHAPTER 27

THE ANNOUNCEMENT

Camp was just over halfway done. All the campers had their routines down and no one seemed to be getting lost anymore, except for the one kid in the Cherokee tribe, but they said he was never good at listening.

At breakfast that particular morning, Mr. Hendrix announced that a special guest would be giving a lecture after dinner. There was a collective groan from the campers. The hours after their final daily meal were typically reserved for free time. Camper didn't want to miss free time.

"Now hold on, campers," Mr. Hendrix calmed from the table he was standing on. "I think you might like this guest." Chatter drowned out the room. He called for silence again. "Would you like to know who our special guest is?"

A not-so-excited "Yes, Mr. Hendrix," rose from the room. More than a few campers rolled their eyes.

"Drum roll please," said Mr. Hendrix. Campers pounded lightly on their tables. "Our special guest is…Jacee Trevane!"

Almost all the girls in the room squealed in delight. Jacee Trevane! He was only the most popular singer and multi-millionaire in the country, and possibly the world. He'd graced every pre-teen and teen magazine multiple times. His latest song, *'I'll Sing You The Night'*, was smashing all kinds of records on the Billboard charts.

Even the boys in the room talked excitedly to their friends. Jacee Trevane wasn't only a platinum recording artist and producer who sold out huge stadiums around the world, he was also a really great athlete, actor and outdoorsman. He'd turned down scholarships to play football and basketball to sing. Benjamin's dad had even said Trevane was one of the top prospects in the last ten years in both sports.

He also snowboarded with Olympians and surfed with professionals. The year before, Trevane scaled Mt. Everest at the young age of 20.

Add to that, Trevane also did volunteer work all over the globe. There weren't many honest people that could deny Jacee Trevane's worth to the world.

"There's one more surprise!" Mr. Hendrix shouted over the din. The campers diverted their attention back to the director. "Some of you may know that Mr. Trevane gives a lot of money and spends a lot of time with kids your age. For some reason we were lucky enough to be picked by his newest charity. There may be people filming…"

Girls squealed again.

"…and Mr. Trevane will be selecting one lucky camper to go on a half day hike with him and his crew."

All sense in the room was lost. One of them would be picked to spend almost a whole day with Jacee Trevane! It was a once in a lifetime…no, once in twenty lifetimes chance.

Mr. Hendrix had to pull out his megaphone and press the siren button. Campers clamped hands over their ears as Mr. Hendrix smiled. The wailing stopped.

"So, everyone's name has been put into a bucket and Mr. Trevane will personally select one slip and announce the winner after he talks to you tonight."

There was no quieting the crowd this time. Two girls fainted. Four boys danced on their table. The noise was almost as deafening as Mr. Hendrix's siren. Waving to his counselors, he motioned for them to escort their tribes out.

CHAPTER 28

JACEE TREVANE

Counselors struggled to maintain order the entire day. The only thing anyone was talking about was Jacee Trevane. Some of the boys had even ditched class to practice some of Trevane's hit songs in the off chance that they might be able to audition for him. Jacee Trevane wasn't only a superstar, he also made stars.

Even Benjamin got caught up in the excitement. He'd never seen a celebrity before. Benjamin was curious to see what Jacee Trevane would be like.

The day dragged on and on for the campers. Even the youngest girls primped and pranced. The boys put on the coolest clothes their parents had packed.

Finally the time came. All the campers gathered around the campfire. Earlier in the day some of the film crew arrived and installed better lighting around the campfire. With the flick of a switch, the area would look almost like it was daytime.

At precisely eight o'clock, Jacee Trevane made his entrance. Tall and athletically thin, he was wearing a pair of stylish yet rugged jeans, a vintage t-shirt and cowboy boots. Flashing his famous smile on his boyishly handsome face, Trevane worked the crowd. Pandemonium ensued. Girls cried. Boys yelled 'Jacee!' The camp counselors struggled to keep the kids back.

Trevane took it in stride. He laughed and waved to the crowd. After a couple minutes of shaking hands with the kids on the front rows, Trevane walked back to where Mr. Hendrix waited with his bull horn. He handed it to Trevane.

"Hello, Camp Wahamalican!"

His wide smile looked sincere as he waited for the screams to die down. He motioned with his hands for the last yellers to quiet down. They did as commanded.

"First, I wanted to thank Mr. Hendrix and the rest of the camp staff for having me," the video cameras manned by Trevane's crew panned side to side, taking in the crowd's reaction. "Next, I wanted to thank you campers for giving up some of your free time to listen to a dork like me." He made a pouty face and girls' shrieks filled the clearing again. Trevane smiled. He was a pro.

"So let me tell you a little bit about why I'm here. You see, I always loved summer camp…"

Trevane went on to tell about how some of favorite memories were from camp. Now that he had more influence, he wanted to make sure as many kids as possible had the chance to experience the same thing. Benjamin listened intently especially when Trevane mentioned his anti-bullying organization.

"There's no reason anyone should get bullied," Trevane explained. "I was bullied when I was your age, and it hurt." He told two stories about times he'd been harassed by other boys in school. "Great camps like the one we're standing in now foster a sense of brother and sisterhood. We need to be kind to each other. Do you understand what I'm saying?"

"YEEEEEEEES!!!" the crowd yelled.

Trevane chuckled. "Good. Now, as some of you may know, I love to do things outdoors. One of my favorites is hiking. Who here likes hiking?"

Every hand in crowd shot up. No one wanted displease the amiable superstar.

"Would anyone like to go for a little hike with me tomorrow?"

"YEEEEEEEES!" screamed the ecstatic campers.

"Okay, okay. If you can all quiet down one more time Mr. Hendrix is gonna bring out that bucket with all your names in it. I'll pick one lucky winner to come with me tomorrow."

Mr. Hendrix made a big show of carrying the white cleaning bucket up to the celebrity. He shook it as he walked and mixed it with his hand. Mr. Hendrix extended the bucket to Jacee. Trevane closed his eyes and stuck a hand in taking his time, letting the tension build. Campers held their breath. The only sound in the clearing were the crunchy steps of the camera crew on the dry grass and the crackling of the orange fire.

Trevane extracted his hand which was now balled in a fist.

"Are you ready to find out who the winner is?" he asked with a crooked eyebrow.

"YEEEEEES!!!"

Trevane handed the bullhorn back to Mr. Hendrix and lowered his balled hand. He slowly opened his hand, palm facing in, picked the small piece of folded white paper with two fingers, and opened it.

"The person spending a day with me tomorrow is… BENJAMIN DRAGON!"

<hr />

Benjamin vaguely remembered being pushed up to the front of the crowd to meet the world famous Jacee Trevane. He hadn't heard the crying of the girls who had lost their one chance of spending time with their crush. He hadn't seen the angry glares from jealous boys who lost their shot of hanging out with their idol.

After the drawing, Trevane had one of his people bring out an acoustic guitar. Luckily, that calmed the hysterical campers. They sat and listened for close to an hour as *The* Jacee Trevane played song after song with just a guitar just ten feet from their faces.

Benjamin didn't hear one note. He sat in stunned silence among his fellow Tomahawks. They guarded him (especially Nathan) like a celebrity. Somehow Trevane's influence had transferred in some part to him. Benjamin didn't know what to think.

Other than academic awards, he'd never won anything in his life. Part of him was excited. Another part of him hated being in the spotlight. He always got tongue-tied in front of a crowd. Would it be the same way with Trevane? Would they walk for half a day without saying a word?

Benjamin's face was pale and his hands were clammy. No one seemed to notice. Not even Nathan. The rest of the people gathered around the fire fixated on the melodic genius of Jacee Trevane. They swayed when he swayed. They smiled when he smiled. They cried when his songs were sad.

And Benjamin? Benjamin sat in his own scared world dreading the next day.

CHAPTER 29

THE HIKE

Much to Benjamin's dismay, the sun did rise the next morning. He forced himself to eat a slice of toast at breakfast and took a single quivering sip of water. Nathan and Aaron had to shoo away boys and girls that kept coming to their table with napkins, dolls and pictures to give to Benjamin so he could get them signed by Jacee. If Benjamin noticed, he didn't make a sign. Nathan waved a hand in front of Benjamin's face.

"Anybody in there?" he asked.

"What? Uh yeah. I'm just tired," said Benjamin, his face sagging.

"You sure you're okay? I heard you moving a lot in your sleep last night." Concern etched Nathan's normally happy face.

"No, I'm okay."

Nathan didn't look convinced. He looked up at the dining hall clock with its crooked minutes hand.

"It's almost time, Dragon."

Benjamin's face somehow turned an even muddier white. His stomach churned again. He was not looking forward to the hike.

———◆———

Benjamin waited at the appointed spot with Mr. Hendrix and two other counselors he didn't know. They hadn't let Nathan come along despite his protests.

"Mr. Trevane's assistant said they'll have food and water for you, Benjamin," said Mr. Hendrix. "You look a little woozy. Don't worry, Mr. Trevane is very down to earth for a celebrity. Besides, I don't think they'll be taking a very hard trail."

On cue, a black SUV with black rims pulled up next to them. Jacee Trevane, outfitted in a rugged t-shirt, olive drab shorts and hiking boots, hopped out of the vehicle first. He looked like a kid on Christmas morning.

"Good morning, Mr. Hendrix, Benjamin."

They all shook hands and stepped over to where Trevan's crew was divvying up camera gear and supplies. It looked like they'd come well stocked. Not that Benjamin noticed or cared. He was trying to keep his knees from knocking together.

Jacee snagged a small backpack and handed it to Benjamin.

"Here you go, buddy. Packed it myself. Got a couple bottles of water, some trail mix and a couple candy bars."

"Uh, thanks," answered Benjamin in a raspy voice. His throat felt dry and scratchy.

"No problem." He turned to his crew. "You guys ready?"

"Yes, sir," one of the assistants answered.

Trevane grabbed one of the large backpacks by the sides, flipped it over his head, and slid his arms through the straps.

"Let's go!" said Trevane, with a look of pure joy.

———

They started out at a leisurely pace. Benjamin didn't have a problem keeping up. It didn't take him long to warm up to Jacee. Trevane seemed genuinely interested in everything about Benjamin like where he was from, what he liked in school, if he played any sports, etc…Not even an hour into the hike, Benjamin was smiling and joking with the superstar. Benjamin soaked up the beauty of the densely wooded landscape. It was a perfect day to be out. Not too hot and not too cold. He'd even forgotten about the cameras filming their journey.

Jacee told Benjamin that they were hiking up to a lookout he'd heard about. Supposedly it overlooked a huge area and afforded an awesome view. Trevane's eyes sparkled as he talked about the other treks he'd been on. Not once did he make Benjamin feel that this hike was beneath him.

They occasionally took short breaks for water and snacks. Trevane told Benjamin that it was better to eat small portions more often instead of pigging out when you stopped. He said it helped keep a hiker's body 'on-level', whatever that meant.

It surprised Benjamin how easily the conversation flowed from his mouth. He found himself telling Trevane all about the places he'd lived and what his mom and dad did for a living. Trevane was particularly curious about Mr. Dragon's football career since he'd played as well. It turned out they'd both played the same position, quarterback.

"You know, before I started playing football I was about your size. I used to get picked on all the time. That's why I started my no bullying foundation. It kills me to hear some of the stories from kids we've helped. Have you ever been bullied?" asked Trevane.

"Yeah."

Trevane nodded solemnly.

"Sucks, huh?"

"Yeah."

"I know it's hard, Benjamin, but it will get better. You can't imagine it now, I know, but it will."

They both walked silently for a bit until Trevane looked back to his film crew.

"You guys mind shutting down for a few minutes. We should be there soon. I wanted to have a private talk with Benjamin."

The tall sandy haired assistant moved to protest. Trevane put up a hand that silenced any objections. He was the boss. The videographers stopped taping and hung back. The rest followed suit.

"Come on, dude," Trevane grinned at Benjamin. "Race you to the top!"

Benjamin smiled and took off down the path with Trevane right behind.

Benjamin gasped for breath as they broke out of the woods and took in the elevated view. Small puffy clouds dotted the sapphire sky. They could see for miles and miles in all directions.

Trevane stripped his pack off and set it on the ground.

"Woooohooooo!" he yelled over the cliff. Now he really looked like a kid on Christmas morning.

Benjamin followed Trevane's lead and took off his new backpack. He closed his eyes and inhaled the summer air with its hints of jasmine and honeysuckle.

"Pretty cool, huh?" asked Trevane.

"Yeah."

"Let's grab a seat." Trevane pointed at the large rock sitting near the edge of the drop-off.

They both clambered up onto the rock and found a comfortable spot over-looking the vista. Benjamin kept as far back from the edge as he could. He wasn't the biggest fan of heights.

"So, Benjamin, you thought about what you wanna be when you grow up?" Trevane said it half serious and half jokingly. How many ten-year-olds knew what they wanted to be when they grew up?

"Not really."

Jacee nodded. "No thoughts about becoming a singer?" A sly smile crept onto his face, teasing.

"No way. I get too nervous standing in front of a bunch of people."

"Most people do. You know what the secret is?"

Benjamin shook his head and took a drink from his water bottle.

"Pretend that everyone in the audience is naked!"

Benjamin almost spit his water all over Jacee. He managed to cup a hand over his mouth and the water ricocheted onto his own shirt. They both laughed.

"Seriously though, getting up in front of people takes a lot of practice. I didn't like it much at first either."

Benjamin's eyes widened. "Really?"

"Yep. I started doing shows when I was really young. Back then my Mom made me do it."

"Do you still like it?"

"I do, actually."

"That's cool."

"You don't sound convinced."

Benjamin shrugged and looked toward the horizon. "Doesn't it get pretty tiring? I don't know if I could do that."

"There are some hard days. I do get to do a lot of good though. I have my own plans for the future though."

Something about his tone made Benjamin turn and look back at the handsome pop star.

"What kinda plans?"

Trevane stared off into the sky. Without looking at Benjamin he answered.

"I've got a lot of influence now. Everyone still looks at me like a kid. They have no idea what I'm capable of."

The edge in his voice sent a chill up Benjamin's spine. Jacee's demeanor had hardened along with the tone of the conversation. Benjamin wished the rest of the hiking party was with them.

Trevane looked back at the young boy, his eyes softening and a smile reclaiming its place.

"Do you know why I came to visit your camp?" he asked.

"For your no bullying thing, right?" Benjamin was afraid he'd answered incorrectly.

"That was part of it. I'm also looking for something."

"What?"

"Well, not technically something. Actually I'm looking for someone."

"Whoare you looking for?"

Trevane offered his best magazine smile. "I was looking for you, Benjamin Dragon."

CHAPTER 30

PROPOSITIONS

Benjamin didn't know how to answer. Was Trevane being serious? Benjamin held his breath waiting for the punch line of the joke. None came.

"B..but the drawing," stammered Benjamin.

Trevane waived the thought away like he was getting rid of a pesky gnat.

"It was always going to be you, Benjamin."

Trevane's face had changed subtlety. Most kids probably wouldn't had notice it. Benjamin did because he'd made a habit of learning facial expressions since he was little. Since he couldn't read emotions through what people said he'd found that reading their faces was more accurate. Trevane looked like a man in his element. He resembled a proud hunter that had finally captured a prized lion.

"Why me?" Benjamin choked out.

Trevane laughed and looked at his watch. "I'll keep this short because my team will be here soon. They don't know anything about this and you'd be smart not to tell them or anyone else about this conversation." He paused to make sure Benjamin understood. "I know all about your gift, Benjamin."

Benjamin inhaled sharply. Warning bells rang in his head threatening to destroy his composure. How could Trevane know?

"Let me guess. Kennedy came to see you before camp?"

Fear filled Benjamin's eyes.

"How do you…"

"Oh, Kennedy came to see me a few years ago too. Back then my career was just taking off. One day he shows up at one of my concerts and tells me the same thing he probably told you. Destroyers, healers, blah, blah, blah."

"Are you…"

"A destroyer? Yeah I am."

Benjamin didn't know whether to be scared or relieved. Trevane's cold vibe hadn't changed.

"I mentioned plans a minute ago. Have you watched the news lately? All the war. All the death. We have people in power all over the world that have no idea what they're doing. I want to change that. It won't be overnight. I've already started laying the groundwork. Everyone loves what I stand for. I get access to almost anywhere I want. I've met most of the leaders of the countries that really matter." He paused to flick a tick off his forearm. It seemed symbolic somehow.

"So why were you looking for me?"

Trevane chuckled huskily.

"Let's just say I don't really believe in Kennedy's way. I think there's a better way. Right now the rest of our kind are reactive. They *wait* for something to happen. I say we *start* making things happen. It's time for the world to know that there another power capable of keeping them safe and happy.

In order to do that, I need more people like me. Do you understand the power that we have?"

Without warning Trevane sprang up and jumped off the cliff. It was so fast that Benjamin barely had a chance to catch himself from falling. He was so surprised he didn't even scream.

A second later a grinning Trevane levitated up and over the lip of the cliff. He landed gently on the large rock, his arms crossed smugly.

"You see? I'll bet you didn't know you'd be able to do that!"

Panicky eyes searched for help. There was no way Benjamin wanted to jump off a cliff. Was this all a test? Trevane read his mind.

"Don't worry," he soothed. "It'll be a while before you can do that. I just wanted to show you one of the many things we can do. So what do you say? Want to be like me? I can teach you. I can train you. Just think, you'll never be bullied again. You'll never have to worry about finding friends."

Benjamin looked queasy again. It sounded tempting. He'd never dreamed that something like that was possible. Him friends with Jacee Trevane? What could it hurt?

Before he could answer, a voice sounded from the way they'd come.

"Leave him alone, Jacee."

They both turned to see Wally Goodfriend strolling up with an ornately carved walking stick. His face was clouded and serious.

"I was wondering if you were going to show up, Wally," said Trevane. "I thought you would've been at the camp."

"Got caught helping a family of beavers last night. Didn't get the message from Kennedy until this morning when I got back."

Benjamin looked between the two men surprise registering on his face.

"Well, you just missed our little chat. I think Benjamin will be fine. Feel free to head home." Trevane waved a dismissal.

"I don't think so." Wally spread his feet and stomped his walking stick on the hard-packed ground.

Trevane's eyes narrowed and his smile turned into a tight frown.

"Why don't we let the kid decide?" Trevane looked down at Benjamin who by now was looking at his feet trying to pretend he was somewhere else.

"I think you'd better head back to camp, Jacee," suggested Wally. His face was as serious as Benjamin had ever seen it.

Who was Benjamin supposed to believe? If he was to believe Jacee his life would change in unimaginable ways. He could be *someone*.

If he sided with Wally, his path was still uncertain. His mind wandered as he imagined what the always decisive Nathan would do. Would he have to leave home?

The decision was made not by Benjamin, Trevane or Wally. Instead the film crew emerged from another wooded trail fifty yards away with cameras rolling. Trevane immediately plastered a grin on his expression. "I was wondering where you guys had gone!" he yelled good-naturedly.

"Got a little turned around back there," said the lead assistant. "You told us to take a left at the fork."

"Sorry about that," said Trevane. "I must've gotten my wires crossed."

The film crew stopped when they noticed Wally standing off to the side. One of Trevane's security staff stepped around the rest of the group to get a better vantage point and assess whether the large man was a threat to his boss.

"Don't worry, Johnny," Trevane calmed. "We just met Wally. He lives up here and saw us passing by. Thought he'd come say hello. Nice guy. Helps out at the camp sometimes, right, Wally?"

Wally nodded and tried to soften his features. He knew how imposing his massive frame could be. "Didn't mean to startle you folks. It's like Mr. Trevane said. Was just out for my daily stroll when I happened to see them up here. Just being neighborly," answered Wally with a tense smile.

The security guy relaxed along with the rest of Trevane's entourage.

"How about we all get back. Benjamin here tells me he doesn't want to miss any of his afternoon classes."

Benjamin knew the last comment had been for the benefit of the cameras. He hadn't said anything about wanted to get back. In fact, he'd rather stay where they were and continue the conversation with Wally and Jacee.

———

They'd said goodbye to Wally before heading back down the hiking trail. Although the big man had gone Benjamin could've sworn he kept seeing glimpses of his friend in the woods.

Trevane didn't seem to notice and spent the return trip joking and chatting as if nothing had happened. Benjamin tried to play along but his thoughts were elsewhere. Was this little adventure a part of his chosen path?

After returning to camp greeted by the cheers of campers happy to see their idol, Jacee thanked the staff and Benjamin for the hike.

"I'll have to tell all my friends about it. Maybe they'll come with me next time!" said Jacee.

As he said his goodbyes, Trevane shook Benjamin's hand. There was something in it. He bent down to Benjamin's height. In a voice only the ten-year-old could hear he said, "Remember what I told you, Benjamin. We could do BIG things together. Think about it. That's my card. It has my personal cell phone number on it. Call me when you get home."

Benjamin looked down at the thick white business card in his hand. I was blank except for *Jacee Trevane* printed on one side and a handwritten phone number on the other. A thrill of excitement coursed through his body.

"Thanks, Jacee."

"No problem, Buddy."

He patted Benjamin on the back, turned, bowed to the crowd and hopped in the black SUV. As they drove off Benjamin was mobbed by fellow campers anxious to hear about his once in a lifetime experience. Little did they know that the hike would be just the beginning.

CHAPTER 31

END OF CAMP

For two days, Benjamin lived like a celebrity. Girls touched him for no reason. Boys asked to be in pictures with him. He reluctantly accepted the adulation.

Luckily he'd remembered to get Trevane to sign a couple things for his friends. He particularly cherished the look on Emily's face when he handed her a smooth river rock signed by the famous singer.

"Thank you so much, Benjamin!" she squealed and hugged him.

He wished he had a thousand more signed river rocks for Emily.

The excitement died down gradually. Nathan somehow made it known that his friend no longer wanted to be bothered. The few people that didn't get the hint were shooed away by either Nathan or Aaron.

They were nearing the end of camp and everyone was trying to soak up their last bits of freedom.

Benjamin visited Wally two more times before leaving for home. The first visit felt awkward. Neither one knew quite what to say and just sat in front of the fire sipping steaming cups of hot chocolate.

During the second visit, Wally's mood lightened. It made Benjamin feel better. He thought he'd done something wrong. Benjamin was curious about the confrontation on the hilltop.

"So what's Jacee all about, Wally?"

The large healer huffed and threw another log on the fire. Sparks flew as the wood bounced and then settled.

"We've been keeping an eye on him for a while. I won't tell you he's a bad kid…it's just that we get the feeling that he's up to no good."

"Like how?"

Wally stared into the fire, his features twisting in contemplation.

"I probably shouldn't…I just…Kennedy would be really mad if I told you."

"Told me what?"

"Now that's enough about that. I don't even know everything. How about you ask Kennedy about it the next time you see him?"

And with that Wally changed the subject and dodged further questioning.

They ended the visit promising to stay in touch. Benjamin scribbled his email address on a faded yellow lined pad sitting on the kitchen table. Wally did the same and ripped it off and gave it to Benjamin.

"Now you take care, okay?" said Wally, offering his hand.

"I will," Benjamin promised, shaking the hand that was three times the size of his own.

—▪—

Summer camp ended all too soon. The final camp fire was filled by skits by campers and staff. One of the favorites was when campers impersonated camp staff. One boy did a hilarious impression of Mr. Hendrix manning his bull horn. Even Mr. Hendrix laughed until his stomach hurt.

The next morning new friends cried as they said their goodbyes. Tribe mates signed the backs of the tribe pictures they'd taken earlier in camp. Nathan wrote something funny on his fellow Tomahawk's pictures. Benjamin just wrote, *'See you next summer, Benjamin.'*

Mrs. Dragon and Mrs. Pratt arrived in a flurry of hugs and kisses.

"My goodness! You boys look like you've grown a foot!" exclaimed Mrs. Pratt.

When they were finally able to pry their moms off, the two boys made their last trip to the camp store. Nathan only had five dollars left in his account and spent it on a camp postcard and some candy. Benjamin was surprised to see that he still had almost one hundred dollars left in his account. He looked at Nathan who grinned back.

Ten minutes later, the two boys emerged with matching rabbit skin pelts, rabbit's feet, camp coins, small bags of fake snakes and loads of candy, of course.

"You boys ready?" asked Mrs. Dragon.

Benjamin and Nathan looked at each other and nodded with suddenly droopy dispositions. Goodbye Camp Wahamalican!

CHAPTER 32

BACK TO REALITY

Benjamin sat on his bed twirling Jacee's business card in his hand. He hadn't moved from the spot in close to an hour. His cell phone sat ready beside him on a pillow.

He'd been home for almost a week. After the final talk with Wally, he thought for sure Kennedy would have called, emailed, something! What was he supposed to do?

Frustration and impatience was making him grumpy. Even his dad had noticed. It didn't help that he was bored. Compared to the constant activity at camp, summer life at home was downright dull.

Benjamin looked at the handwritten number one last time then rose from his mussed bed and repined the card in the middle of the corkboard next to his desk.

"He probably wouldn't remember me anyway," he muttered.

———◆———

After a snack of crackers and cheese, Benjamin decided to go for a walk. He would've asked Nathan to come with him if he didn't have to work at his dad's shop during the day to pay back the money for camp. Aaron was out of town with his parents and Emily was busy at dance camp.

With his parents at work all day, Benjamin was left on his own. Mr. and Mrs. Dragon knew he wouldn't get into trouble. He hadn't before. They trusted him to stick close to home and call if he needed anything.

Benjamin shoved his cell phone in a pocket and left out the garage door. He could get back in by entering a code that would open the automatic door.

Not really having a destination Benjamin headed in the general direction of the small town center. Maybe he'd stop in at the little hobby shop. There were a bunch of cool things to look at. Besides, he had money burning a hole in his pocket. He'd hoarded his weekly allowance for months. Maybe there would be a new model airplane or metal figurine he could buy. He liked the ones that were molded into fire-breathing dragons, of course.

———

The hobby shop only had a couple people roaming around. Benjamin walked in and let the cool air conditioning sweep over his body. He'd worked up a sweat just walking there. It was getting midsummer hot outside.

He spent a few minutes perusing the aisles looking to see if there was anything new since the last time he'd been in. Stopping at a large glass case next to another boy his age, Benjamin peered in. There were two opposing armies of painted metal figurines lined and ready for battle. One side had knights, archers and a king and queen. The other had orcs, goblins, trolls and a dragon.

Benjamin always thought it was interesting that dragons were on the bad side in most stories. Why couldn't there be more good dragons…like him?

———◆———

He left the craft shop after paying for his new model M1A1 Abrams tank and miniature dragon. At least it would give him something to do for a day or two. Benjamin thought about painting the dragon red before adding it to his collection. He had nine others hidden in an old box in his bedroom closet. Maybe it was time to take them out and put them on display.

———◆———

Without even realizing where he was going, Benjamin looked up and noticed he'd somehow made it to the park he and Nathan liked to hang out at. It gave him an idea.

He found a secluded spot and sat down. There were a couple parents with kids at the jungle gym, but they were talking or checking their phones.

Benjamin decided to start easy. He picked a blade of grass and held it in his palm. After closing his eyes and taking a deep breath he focused on the one-inch piece of greenery. He stared and stared. He tried to will it to move. He whispered, "Float." Nothing. No movement. Not even a flutter.

Wally said it took practice. Benjamin silently promised himself that he would practice each and every day. That way whenever he chose his path his 'gift' would be ready to be used.

Taking another steadying breath Benjamin refocused on the object in his hand. This time, instead of trying to make the grass move, he pretended he was the grass. A second later he felt a funny sensation. The grass hadn't moved so he looked around. He was floating a foot off the ground!

His surprise was complete. As quick as it had happened, it ended. Benjamin's rear thumped down onto the ground. He hastily looked around to see if anyone had noticed. No one had.

Grabbing his shopping bag, Benjamin made the wise decision that maybe practicing in the privacy of his fenced-in backyard would be better. Excited about the prospect, he ran all the way home.

Benjamin grabbed a glass of ice water on his way out the back door. Finding a quiet spot on the grass underneath a weeping willow, he sat down anxiously. A couple deep breaths got his heartbeat under control. He now knew how Jacee had levitated. It was simply a matter of making *himself* float like the object. In a roundabout way he could fly, but not really. It should be simple.

Closing his eyes, Benjamin imagined himself rising. He peeked once through squinted eyes. Still on the ground. Next he thought of things that were light like feathers or balls of cotton. He tried to make his body just as weightless. Nothing.

He thought that maybe if he fully relaxed it would be easier so he laid down on his back with arms spread wide. A bird singing in the tree distracted him. The red breasted sparrow chirped and quipped ignoring him completely. Still he couldn't make himself rise in the air.

Benjamin thought back to what he was thinking about when it had happened at the park. The grass!

He sat up and pulled a dark green strand of grass. Holding it in his hand he closed his eyes hoping it would work. It did! A second later he was floating lightly in the air. He had a better grasp of it this time. Instead of plunking down he controlled his thoughts and easily glided around the yard a foot above the grass.

At one point he spun himself around so fast that he almost lost control. He laughed at the feeling. His body parts still felt normal. It wasn't like what he'd read in books. He was simply willing his own body in a way he'd never thought possible.

It was time to try something harder. While still floating, Benjamin focused his attention on a small rock a few feet away. He didn't get it the first time and knocked his tailbone pretty good when he dropped down.

Making his body rise was effortless this time. He didn't even need the piece of grass. Sitting in the air cross-legged, Benjamin allowed part of his mind to keep him in the air while focusing another part of his brain to lift the rock. It kind of felt like that old trick where you pat your head and rub your belly at the same time. Benjamin figured he could do the same with his gift.

This time it did work. The stone rose slowly and moved to Benjamin's silent command bobbing and twirling as if on a string.

"Benjamin!" came the call from inside. It was Mrs. Dragon. Benjamin and the rock fell unceremoniously back to earth. He rubbed his rear from the repeated thumps.

"I'm in the back, mom!" he called back.

A moment later Mrs. Dragon opened the back door.

"What are you doing back here, honey?" she asked.

"Oh, just…hanging out."

CHAPTER 33

A SURPRISE GUEST

That night Benjamin scarfed down his dinner in record time and excused himself. Mrs. Dragon glanced at him with raised eyebrows. She'd barely taken a second bite of her kale salad in the time it had taken him to shovel the entire heaping bowl of penne pasta into his mouth.

"Got somewhere to be, honey?"

"I got a model tank at the store today. Is it okay if I go upstairs and build it?" asked Benjamin, trying to hide his excitement.

"Let's not stay up too late tonight okay? I think you need to get back on your routine. Camp got you staying up past your normal bed time. I don't want you sleepy all day."

"Okay, mom."

He cleared his plate, kissed his surprised mother on the cheek, and ran upstairs.

After taking the parts out of the small model box and arranging them on his desk, Benjamin set on his real task. More practice.

He had the hang of it now. Pencils twirled and paper tumbled. Pillows floated and shoes flipped. There wasn't a thing in his room that he couldn't move with his mind. At one point he had nine things floating in unison. He even made them dance like the he'd seen in Cinderella when the fairy godmother used her magic and that whole Bippity Boppoty Something.

It was too bad he couldn't tell anyone. Even Nathan had luckily seemed to forget about his gift. He thought about writing Wally on the computer. In the end it was all too much fun. The objects in his room continued to be his guinea pigs. Marveling at the way he could make them go as fast or as slow as he wanted, Benjamin didn't even hear his mom's steps until it was almost too late. Just as the door creaked open he willed the five army men he'd had marching across the room, in the air, of course, to fall to the ground.

"Time to go to bed."

Mrs. Dragon stepped in the room and looked around at the mess on the floor. Benjamin turned his head and pretended to be fiddling with his pillow case.

"What's going on in here?" asked Mrs. Dragon.

"I was just, uh, playing, mom."

"I thought you were putting your new tank together."

"Changed my mind. I think I'll do it tomorrow."

Mrs. Dragon walked over and planted a kiss on her son's forehead.

"Alright, but make sure you clean this mess up before you go to bed. And don't forget to brush your teeth."

"Okay."

"Goodnight, Benjamin," she smiled and retired to her own bedroom.

After rushing to clean up his room (it was a lot easier now that he could make his things go where he wanted), changing into his pajamas, and brushing his teeth, he jumped into bed.

He looked at the overhead light switch and made it flip down. This gift thing was gonna be pretty cool.

Benjamin closed his eyes and imagined the possibilities. As he drifted off to sleep his thoughts were of soaring through the clouds…like a dragon.

Waking up earlier than his mom the next morning, Benjamin spooned a bowlful of cereal into his mouth and watched the Cartoon Network. He'd worked out a plan to practice for the day. Now he just had to wait for his mom to leave for work. Mrs. Dragon finally emerged from her bedroom decked out in her usual grey pant suit. She had her hair tied back in a ponytail the way her husband liked it. Mr. Dragon said he liked to see her beautiful neck.

The sight of the ponytail made Benjamin think about Emily. He remembered the ponytail she was wearing when…

"I said good morning."

Benjamin had been so engrossed in his daydream that he hadn't realized his mom was talking.

"Morning, mom."

"You're up early today. Big plans?"

"Not really. Just hanging out again. Probably putting my tank together," said Benjamin as nonchalantly as he could.

Mrs. Dragon eyed her son like she was trying to figure out whether he was telling the truth.

"Well alright, but make sure you eat a good lunch. I left you some money if you want to get some pizza."

"Can I get you anything for breakfast, mom?"

Mrs. Dragon stopped packing her bag and looked up.

"Up early AND being helpful? Is that my son over there or should I call NASA because some alien took over his body?"

"Very funny, Mom," he said, rolling his eyes.

Mrs. Dragon grabbed a protein shake and stuffed it in her briefcase.

"Call me if you need anything, okay? It'll be a late night a work. I'll call when I know what time I'll be home."

Benjamin's ears perked up. With his dad being out of town and his mom working late, he'd have plenty of time to practice and come up with new ways to use his gift.

After hugging his mom and watching her drive away, Benjamin bolted out the back door eager to get to work himself.

Benjamin soon found that moving objects was a lot like what he imagined a band conductor's job to be like. He had to make sure to keep note of each individual piece while at the same time focusing on the whole. It got easier and easier the more times he tried it.

By lunchtime, he was making patterns of dirt and grass in the air. He wasn't a very good artist, but he could still mold them into shapes like stick figures, simple houses and even a droopy bellied dog.

After his stomach growled for the fifth time, Benjamin stood up and headed to the kitchen. As he was whipping together a peanut butter and banana sandwich the doorbell rang.

Benjamin scooted to the front door, looked through the spy hole…and almost fainted.

―――

Jacee Trevane could see the darkness pass across the outside of the peephole. He waved and smiled.

Benjamin crouched down and rested his back against the door taking deep calming breaths. His heart was beating a million times a minute! Not really, but that's what he thought.

"Benjamin, it's Jacee."

Benjamin didn't know what to do. His mom and dad always told him not to let strangers in the house. But was Jacee really a stranger? He thought about calling his mom. He thought about calling his dad. What about Nathan?

In the end he stood shakily and opened the door.

"Hey, Benjamin!"

"Uh, hi, Jacee," replied Benjamin in the most confident voice he could muster. He glimpsed the sleek black convertible sports car parked at the curb. "I'm not supposed to let strangers in."

Jacee bobbed his head in agreement. "Smart. Would it be okay if we took a walk? I was just in the area and wanted to stop in and say hello." There was no trace of deception in his voice. He sounded genuinely happy to see Benjamin.

"Ummm…"

"You can call your parents if you want. I don't want you to get in trouble."

Benjamin thought about it. On one hand his parents would be even more surprised that superstar, rockstar, awesome dude Jacee Trevane was coming to visit him. On the other hand, they probably wouldn't like him to be hanging out with without adult supervision.

He shook his head. "No, it's okay. Let me get my phone and I'll meet you in front of the garage."

Jacee nodded and headed to the garage.

Benjamin locked the front door and sighed. His day had been perfect until that moment. But…just maybe Trevane could give him some more tricks. Buoyed by the thought he skipped through the house, locked the back door, grabbed his phone from the kitchen table and headed out through the empty garage.

Jacee was waiting patiently, reading something on his cell phone.

"Ready?" asked Trevane.

Benjamin nodded.

They took a meandering course around the neighborhood. Luckily, there weren't other kids around or they'd probably mob the celebrity and ask for his autograph. Jacee asked him about how the rest of camp had gone and Benjamin told him.

After a few blocks, the good-looking celeb asked the question that Benjamin had been dreading.

"Have you thought about what we talked about on our hike?"

"Yeah."

"And...?"

"I...I don't know. I was wondering if you could tell me some more."

"What do you want to know?"

Benjamin scoured his mind for the next couple paces. Just like his meeting with Old Kennedy, he had a thousand things he wanted to ask Jacee.

"Why me?" Benjamin asked.

"I want someone who's just come into their gift. The old timers are, well, old. They've got a different way of looking at things. I think we need a new breed. We need to be willing to change the world, not just sit back and react to what's happening."

Benjamin stared ahead as he digested the information. It would be fun to be part of something new.

"Why don't Wally and Kennedy want to be a part of this?"

Jacee snorted.

"They've got their own ideas. They're happy to sit on the sidelines. I want to act and they don't get that. Honestly I think it scares them. Me, I'm not afraid. The more of us there are, the more we can change things. The other thing is that they want to stay secret. Now I'm not saying we're gonna start talking to newspapers or anything like that, but I think the world should know that *someone* is doing *something*."

It sounded reasonable. With all the crazy things going on in the world there should be a force for good. Kind of like superheroes, but without the cheesy capes and stuff. Benjamin liked the thought of it.

"So...like, what kind of things would you want to change?"

Jacee spread his arms wide and spun in a quick circle.

"Everything! Image no more war, no more poverty, everyone getting along."

"But, how?"

Jacee's eyes hardened for a flicker of a moment. Benjamin wasn't sure if he'd imagined it.

"We'll make them see."

"See what?"

Jacee's smile widened.

"Can I show you something?"

"Where?"

"I can't tell you that, but I can take you there." There was a mischievous sparkle in Jacee's eyes like he was about to show Benjamin something he wasn't supposed to see.

"I…I don't know."

"Come on, Benjamin! We're both the same. Don't you see that?"

Benjamin wanted to be the same as Jacee. That would mean he'd be popular and famous. Who didn't want that?

"Okay."

"Great. Now this is gonna sound weird, but you're gonna have to hold on to my hands." Jacee extended his arms and Benjamin tentatively did as he was told. Before he could take a breath they rocketed into the air and disappeared from sight.

CHAPTER 34

THE ISLAND

Benjamin squinted against the relentless force of the oncoming air. When he finally got his bearings he saw that they were travelling at a hurtling speed like a missile. It frightened him until he looked up and saw Jacee laughing at his shocked expression. Benjamin forced a smile so Jacee wouldn't think he was some kind of wimp.

They eventually touched down next to a body of water. Benjamin knew it was the ocean from the hot salty air and faint smell of seaweed. It sparkled with countless ripples moving in every direction. A sheer rock wall loomed behind them towering over one hundred feet. It looked like it had been carved by some giant who'd used its hands to scrape the stone away in long strokes. Benjamin squinted. There were images of men, women and animals intertwined in the façade.

"You like it?" Jacee asked, breaking Benjamin's awed silence.

"Like what?"

"You name it, the flight over, the ocean, my art."

Benjamin's face scrunched in confusion. "What art?"

Jacee pointed to the rock wall.

Benjamin's eyes went wide. "You made *that*?"

"Well, I didn't make the rock, but I did carve it. Pretty cool, huh?"

They stood for a moment admiring the impressive piece of modern art. It would have taken a crew of men years to do such a thing. It reminded Benjamin of the time he'd visited Mount Rushmore and seen the faces of American Presidents carved into the side. Mount Rushmore had taken almost fifteen years to shape.

"Pretty cool," repeated Benjamin.

"You stick with me and you'll be doing the same thing in no time."

"Is this what you wanted to show me?"

"Yes and no. The real surprise is up ahead. Come on."

As they walked up the beach, Jacee described the figures he'd carved into the rock wall. He said it had taken him just over a month to complete it in between concerts overseas. There were plans to do the same all over the world. Jacee said it would be his calling card.

"What's a calling card?" Benjamin asked.

"It basically tells people you've been there. Kind of like a mark you make on a tree on trail or a note you leave at someone's house."

Benjamin didn't really understand what his new friend was talking about so he just walked along bobbing his head every now and then. One thing was for sure, Jacee was super serious about whatever he was planning.

After a short walk, they saw streams of smoke in the distance.

"We're almost there," said Jacee, beaming from ear to ear.

"Almost where?"

"I want it to be a surprise," winked Jacee.

Pretty soon the pair made out stone huts and tanned figures walking around. One of them spotted the pair and shouted to the others. In a second there were ten men with spears and loin clothes trotting their way. Benjamin looked to Jacee for guidance. Jacee kept walking as if nothing was wrong.

The men were barefooted and had shaved heads that glistened with sweat in the midday sun. One of the men barked a command in a foreign language and the group halted in the sand.

"Well? What do you think?" asked Jacee.

"Are they…uh, friendly?"

"To us they are."

"Who are they?"

Jacee looked to the warriors and pointed to the ground. Instantly they all knelt and cast their eyes to the ground.

"They're my people."

It was pretty obvious that Jacee was not technically from this place. His lighter skin color was probably the biggest giveaway. "How are they your people?" asked Benjamin.

"I found them one day when I was exploring the islands. They're a very primitive tribe. Until I got to know them they were even cannibals."

Benjamin gulped. "You mean they eat people?"

"They used to. I got them to stop that nasty habit."

"So why are they *your* people?"

"You'll see soon," said Jacee walking toward the kneeling men.

They rose on command and greeting him like some kind of general or president. Benjamin watched. It was curious to see the way the dark-skinned savages bowed in deference to young man. Jacee took it all in stride and looked completely at home. Maybe they knew him from his music and touring too. Benjamin looked around for some sign of modern civilization, but only saw palm trees, jungle and ocean.

———

After being solemnly escorted to the small village and greeted by the women and children of the tribe (Jacee said what they were called, but Benjamin couldn't pronounce it) they were guided to an area overlooking the ocean. There were woven mats neatly arranged on the sand. Jacee didn't hesitate to take the best spot.

Serving women brought several bowls made out of wood and coconut.

"Are we eating here?" Benjamin asked nervously. He didn't like the thought of eating food that wasn't properly prepared. There was no pizza or pasta that he could see.

"We are."

Jacee ignored his young friend and talked to two old men in their native tongue. He didn't seem to have any difficulty understanding them. There was a lot of pointing and grunting that Benjamin didn't understand.

After what seemed like an eternity, and after Benjamin had tried to politely say he didn't want the continued offerings of raw fish and mushy-looking glop, Jacee turned back to him.

"Pretty awesome, right?"

"Yeah. So what are we doing here?"

Villagers watched them as they, or at least Jacee, ate. Occasional someone new would walk up, bow and mouth something silently. There was a feeling of utmost respect in the way they carried themselves around Jacee.

"I stop in from time to time to see if they need anything. They don't get many visitors on the island. When I first showed up they tried to kill me. That was until I showed them my powers."

"You showed them your powers?" whispered Benjamin.

Jacee nodded smugly.

"Of course."

"But, I thought we weren't…"

"Let me guess. Old Man Kennedy told you not to show anyone what you can do."

Benjamin nodded.

Jacee picked up a piece of raw fish with his fingers and popped it in his mouth. He closed his eyes and chewed the food with a contented hum.

"Tell me, Benjamin, what good are our gifts if we can't share them with the world?"

"I don't know," answered Benjamin, like he'd been called out by his teacher for not knowing the correct answer to a math question.

"Let me tell you, it's pretty lame. These powers are amazing things that people want to see, that they *need* to see. Did

you know that the first day I met this tribe I not only deliv-
ered them a school of fish that fed them for months, but I also
made those stone huts over there." Jacee's voice rose. "Before
that they lived in pathetic little huts made of branches and
leaves. Every time a storm blew through they had to run for
the rain forest and when they came back the huts were gone.
I made a difference. *I* gave them a new life."

The two elder tribesmen cowered away slightly at the
sound of Jacee's voice. Benjamin noticed and felt like doing
the same.

"This is what we can do, Benjamin. We can change people's lives and they'll treat us like go…like special benefactors."

Benjamin knew what Jacee meant. He was going to say
people would treat them like gods. To try and hide his unease,
Benjamin picked up a small cone that he hoped held water.
To his relief it was water and he chugged the whole thing in
one breath.

Suddenly there was commotion near the huts. Jacee
scowled and rose from the feast. Benjamin followed his lead
and craned his neck to see what was happening.

"Another wrinkle," he heard Jacee murmer through tight
lips.

Benjamin cocked his head at the comment. What was
going on?

The answer came a moment later when Old Kennedy
strolled into view.

CHAPTER 35

TWO SIDES

"I thought I might find you here," said Kennedy, all humor of their last meeting gone from his face. Instead a look of intense concentration dominated his features.

"So nice of you to join us, Kennedy. I wish you had called and we would've waited to eat."

"I'm not here to eat. I'm here to take the boy back home."

The men stared at each other. Benjamin dropped his gaze to his sand covered sneakers.

"I didn't know you were Benjamin's babysitter. Are the Dragons paying you for that?" Jacee laughed.

"No more games, Trevane. You know I don't approve of this…" he motioned around at the huts and tribe "…charade. It's dangerous and you had no right bringing the boy here."

"I think Benjamin's entitled to make his own decisions. He's a smart kid."

"Benjamin, it's time to go," said Kennedy sternly.

Benjamin glanced at the two men with a look somewhere between embarrassment and fright. Jacee threw his hands up in the air and Kennedy flinched.

"Fine! Take him back if you want. We were almost done anyway."

Kennedy relaxed. Why had he flinched? Did he think that Jacee was going to attack him? Benjamin filed the question away for later.

"Come along, Benjamin," said Kennedy.

Benjamin looked up at Jacee and was surprised to find the confident young man now looking forlorn.

"Thanks for coming with me, Benjamin. I'll be in touch soon."

Benjamin didn't know what to say so he just nodded and followed Kennedy away from the village.

———

The trip back was quiet and seemed to take longer than the first journey. Benjamin didn't know if it was because he felt like he was in trouble or because Old Kennedy just moved them slower through the air than Jacee had. The old man didn't say another word to Benjamin as they floated through clouds and skirted around mountains.

When they arrived, Kennedy set them down in the Dragon's backyard. It wasn't even dark yet. Benjamin couldn't believe he'd travelled so far in so little time.

His mentor sat down on one of the deck chairs. The wrinkles on his face looked more pronounced than they had on the beach. He closed his eyes and sighed.

In a voice barely above a whisper he said, "Come sit with me, Benjamin."

Benjamin did as he was told. Keeping his knees pressed together tightly, he waited patiently for the old man to speak. The feeling of being in trouble lingered and he couldn't shake it.

"I want to apologize, Benjamin."

Benjamin's eyes bulged. Kennedy wanted to apologize to him?

"Okay," was all Benjamin could muster.

"Let me explain. I thought we had more time...I'm getting ahead of myself."

Kennedy reached into his pocket and pulled out an ornately carved wood pipe. He expertly packed it with tobacco and lit it with a match he extracted from another pocket. Benjamin smelled hints of cinnamon and vanilla. After taking a couple puffs, Kennedy continued.

"I know it's probably a nasty habit to you, but I find it calms me. As I was saying...I want to apologize. I fear that I underestimated both you and Mr. Trevane. I assumed that because of your age, I shouldn't give you certain information. Believe me when I say that I was only trying to protect you."

Kennedy inhaled another long pull from his pipe, pursed his lips and blew it out. The smoke streamed out, swirled and took the shape of a question mark. Kennedy smiled.

Benjamin wondered, not for the first time, why adults were always keeping things from kids. They always said it was 'for your own good'. It felt more like lying. Benjamin wasn't stupid and neither were most kids. They knew.

"The last time we chatted I told you about World War Two and the sudden increase of our kind. It was as if nature, the world, God, something, was telling the universe it needed help. We answered that call. It turns out that the same thing may be happening again. None of us know what the threat is, but the increase in gifted youth give us a very real clue that something will happen soon.

"So, I apologize for not relaying the…severity of the situation. It was unfair of me to do so. You had a right to know.

"Next we come to the topic of Mr. Trevane. Wally told me all about the confrontation you three had at camp. I should have been here when you got home. Alas, I was helping to coordinate a mentoring effort in Zimbabwe."

"How did he find out about me?" interrupted Benjamin.

"We aren't sure yet. From what we've been able to gather, Mr. Trevane, as you can imagine, has a vast network of contacts all around the world. Some of those contacts most likely have access to highly classified surveillance technology. We've begun to think that Trevane is having some of us followed and recorded. As we speak, measures are being implemented to thwart further spying attempts by him or any other organization."

"But why me? How did he know where to find me?"

"Finding you was simple. As I said, he has almost limitless technology on his side. His entertainment empire is quite impressive and may even reach into certain foreign government intelligence agencies. As to why he chose you…I am just speculating, but he may have targeted you because you could be easily molded. He did attempt to recruit another young man in Texas. That brave boy chased Mr. Trevane off his property with a shotgun."

"Really?"

Kennedy nodded.

"I hope you'll get to meet Billy sometime soon. He's as tall and as tough as a bull rider, but with a heart of gold."

"How old is he?"

"Ten. Same as you."

Benjamin couldn't imagine chasing Jacee Trevane with a shotgun. He wasn't so sure he'd like to meet Billy.

"Why don't you get along with Jacee?" asked Benjamin.

Kennedy's face dropped slightly and his eyes clouded.

"Jacee Trevane was one of mine. He showed a lot of promise in his early days. His skills doubled overnight. There wasn't anything he couldn't do. Add to that his charismatic presence and you'd think this young boy was someone who could bring our kind into a new generation.

Kennedy shook his head sadly.

"Unfortunately things changed. He didn't like being bound by our rules. His rebellious streak even landed in the newspaper. We were able to spin the tale, but Jacee had made his point. He didn't want to be controlled. Over the years he distanced himself from me. There was always an excuse about why he couldn't meet with me. At first I thought he was just growing up. That was until we started hearing the whispers.

"At that time Jacee had already become a huge star. He was doing a lot of work in poor countries overseas. Well, on one of my journeys to help after a devastating tsunami in the Pacific, I heard whispers from some of the natives. When they didn't know I was listening they wondered why their god had not helped them. At first I thought they were referring to their own god much as Christians do. But then I heard others describe what their *god* looked like. It was the same image every time. There was no mention of a wise man with white hair or even Buddha. They described a young man with white features. Some called him the pale god. I was too busy to investigate, what with the severity of the damage in the area, but when I called on my friends and happened to mention the stories, two others said they'd heard similar reports. Each time it was in a remote area of the world. We put the pieces together and eventually the trail led back to Jacee Trevane."

"But, I don't get it. He said he's trying to help people. Isn't that what he's doing?"

"On the surface, yes. He definitely helps in physical ways. It's what he wants in return that's the problem."

"What does he want?"

"Worship."

"I don't understand," said Benjamin, confusion etched on his face.

"And why would you? You're an innocent boy. You could never imagine wanting people to bow down to you. Yes, it is natural to feel wanted and to feel popular, but Jacee's obsession is something else entirely. Did he tell you that he lost his parents at a young age?"

"I don't think so."

"I'm sure he didn't. It's actually a very important part of the story and quite sad. You see, almost a year after learning about his gift, Jacee had tremendous control. In his mind it was a new toy. He played and experimented. One day while on a camping trip with his parents, Jacee got in an argument with them. I don't know what it was about, and it doesn't matter. What happened next does. Young Jacee threw a fit and stormed off. His mother and father let him go probably thinking he needed time to cool off. You see, even at a young again Jacee had a fiery temper.

"Once he'd gotten a ways off he found a large pile of boulders. Much as a normal child would grab rocks and throw them in a lake or against a wall, Jacee soon found he could lift the huge rocks. It was in the middle of one of the tosses that his parents found him. When he told me the story, tears pouring down his face, Jacee didn't remember exactly what had happened. What I could piece together was that he'd been surprised by his parents mid-throw. The surprise rattled him enough to take his concentration off the boulder. His parents were crushed and died instantly."

Benjamin eyes watered as he imagined the scene. It frightened him. Could he be capable of the same thing? The thought made him shiver.

Kennedy continued.

"Jacee was never the same after that. On the outside he looked like the same care free boy who loved to be onstage. His career progressed, but inside he pulled back. It was all I could do to have a conversation with him. At first he blamed his gift for the tragedy. Then he blamed me. Then he blamed himself. He seemed to get better around age fourteen. I'd kept my distance and waited. By that time he'd cemented his place in history. He was world famous. It was actually Jacee that reached out to me. He apologized and said he wanted to learn more about his gift so he wouldn't hurt anyone else.

"I was so relieved by what he said that I jumped back into his life. For a year I toured with him and when he was home I stayed in his guest cottage. I taught him everything. I told him our history. I told him our rules. He was a good student and picked up most things the first time. Until now he was the smartest and most talented I'd met. That is, until I met you."

"Me?"

"You both have very similar minds. Very bright. Very talented. The only real difference I see is that while he was naturally outgoing you are more reserved and cautious. You asked me earlier why you. I think that's why. He's done his homework and knows how smart you are. School records are effortless for him to hack. He thinks, and rightly so, that your shyness will pass."

"But I'm not anything like him!" Benjamin protested. "He's popular and…I'm…just…"

"You're more alike than you think, Benjamin, and that is what frightens me. Don't you see? He wants to combine your power with his own. He'll train you and mold you. You'll be his. The only thing that could be worse is if you had all three gifts instead of just the one. But as I told you before, that's only happened once in the last two thousand years. You haven't been healing animals while I'm not around have you?" Kennedy gave Benjamin a crooked grin.

"No." Despite the supposed danger Benjamin felt a tiny twang of regret that he wasn't *that* special.

"Good. Now, let's talk about where we go from here."

CHAPTER 36

DECISIONS

Kennedy left before Mr. and Mrs. Dragon returned home. He told Benjamin to think about what they'd discussed and that he'd stop by the next day to answer any questions. They would come up with a plan together.

Benjamin didn't know what to think. Part of him just wanted to go back to being 'normal' again. But that was impossible. His gift wasn't something he could give back.

He didn't say much to his parents at dinner. They were used to it and busied themselves with work, as usual. Benjamin excused himself from the table and went up to his room, barely finding the energy to put one foot in front of the other. The excitement and fear of the day had finally caught up with him. He worried that the distance to his bed might be too far.

Luckily he made it to his room, shut the door and collapsed on his bed. Despite the screams from his body that told him to sleep, Benjamin lay fully awake. Sights and sounds swirled in his mind. The flight to the island. The feel of the clouds gliding through outstretched fingers. Savages with spears. Images carved into a rock face. Deadly boulders.

Exhaustion finally claimed him and Benjamin drifted to sleep on waves as blue as a robin's egg. They were followed by dreams of the future, dreams of greater things to come.

To his great surprise, Benjamin woke early feeling as refreshed as any time he could remember. Maybe it was the prospect of his coming journey. It could've had something to do with his desire to learn how to fly.

He was the first into the kitchen and surprised his mother when she walked in minutes later.

"What are you doing up so early again?" she asked.

"Just wanted to get up, I guess."

"Anything I need to know about?"

"Jeez, Mom. I just wanted to get up early, you know."

"Okay, okay. Sorry."

She left him alone to get a bowl of Greek yogurt and a half of grapefruit. Mr. Dragon walked in a second later.

"Hey, sport! You going to work this morning too?" joked Mr. Dragon.

Mrs. Dragon answered for him.

She shot her husband a knowing look as if to say, 'I think something's up.'

"He's just being more grown up, honey."

Mr. Dragon nodded with a sly grin. He grabbed a banana and took a seat across the table from his son. Benjamin knew what was coming. His dad always had the same look on his face when he was about to play buddy buddy and try to interrogate something out of him.

Before he could lay on the questions, the doorbell rang. Benjamin's stomach tensed.

"I wonder who that could be," wondered Mrs. Dragon, moving toward the front door.

"I'll get it," said Benjamin, with a mouth full of cereal. A pale stream of milk ran out the corner of his mouth. He was already halfway out of his chair.

"You sit and finish your cereal," ordered his mother who walked purposefully to the front hall. The look on her face made it plain that she was not thrilled about having someone ring her doorbell so early in the morning.

A moment later, Benjamin could hear the front door opening and his mom let out an audible gasp.

"I'm so sorry…of course…please come in." It was all they could hear from the distance.

The sound of his mom's heals clicking on the hardwood floor punctuated the thumps in Benjamin's chest. He tried to look nonchalant as Mr. Dragon waited to see who was coming in.

Mrs. Dragon appeared first followed by a familiar figure.

"Benjamin, you didn't tell us you know Mr. Trevane."

Before Benjamin could utter a single syllable, Mr. Dragon was out of his chair extending his hand to Jacee. Benjamin's parents oogled and gushed for a minute. It was so unlike them that were it any one else, Benjamin probably would have laughed. As it was, he was having a hard time swallowing his last bite of cereal. He willed it down and stood on wobbly legs.

"I'm so sorry to barge in like this," said Jacee. "I just happened to be in the neighborhood and wanted to see if Benjamin might like to show me around town today."

His smile melted the normally unflappable Mrs. Dragon. The comment made Mr. Dragon's chest puff with pride for his son.

"Buddy, why didn't you tell us you met Jacee at camp?" asked Mr. Dragon.

Jacee was quick to answer for him. "You know how he is Mr. Dragon…"

"Please call me, Tim."

"…Benjamin isn't a show off. It's one of the reasons we got along so well at camp. I thought he might be able to show me a thing or two about being modest. Besides, we hit it off so well before I thought he might be able to give me some feedback for our new anti-bullying campaign."

Mrs. Dragon almost giggled, but was able to clamp her mouth shut just in time. Mr. Dragon looked at his son and nodded.

"You're right. He may not look like much, but my boy is gonna be something special," bragged Mr. Dragon.

Benjamin just stood with his hands in his pockets wishing he had the gift of invisibility.

Mr. and Mrs. Dragon happily gave their permission for Benjamin to show Jacee the town.

"As long as he's home by dinner time," requested Mrs. Dragon.

"Not a problem. In fact, how about I treat you all to dinner?" offered Jacee.

Benjamin expected his parents to decline citing work or some other well-used excuse. Instead, they both blurted, "Sure!"

It was overcast as they slipped out the front door. Jacee was all smiles and jokes as they said goodbye to Mr. and Mrs. Dragon. That all changed when the house was no longer in site.

Trevane walked without talking. His face had changed. He looked like a person that wanted to say something, but didn't know how to say it. Kind of like having a word or idea on the tip of your tongue and not being able to verbalize it.

Dread prickles crept up the back of Benjamin's head. He didn't want to anger the famous singer so he just kept his mouth shut.

Without warning Jacee whirled to face him, wrath flashing in his eyes. His lips parted like he was going to speak. His eyes focused on something over Benjamin's shoulder and his stormy eyes narrowed more. Instead of speaking he snapped his fingers, grinned and, like a shot, they were both speeding up toward the gray clouds.

Benjamin couldn't see a thing in the smoky cloud cover. The thought of flying into a bird or, even worse, an airplane made him shut his eyes. The flight didn't feel even remotely like the ones the day before. Everything felt wrong. How did Jacee know where they were going if neither of them could see a foot to the front?

Just as the thought came to Benjamin he felt the descent. They were going down. Benjamin braced for landing.

———

Shortly after they touched down. Benjamin opened his eyes and looked around. The landscape looked almost like a barren wasteland. There were a ton of rocks and some scraggly looking trees dotting the area. The next thing Benjamin noted was the heat. They'd only been on the ground for a second and he was already sweating.

"Where are we?" asked Benjamin.

Jacee held up a finger motioning for his young friend to wait.

Seconds later, a third figure landed twenty feet away. It was Kennedy. He was wearing a caramel colored trench coat that flapped languidly in the slight breeze.

"I don't remember inviting you, old man," Jacee sneered.

"I don't recall needing your permission, son."

"Don't call me son. I'm not a kid anymore."

"Very well. This is the last time we're going to do this. I suggest you go back and never contact Benjamin again."

"And what makes you think he wants me to leave?"

"You're right. How about we ask the boy?" suggested Kennedy whose posture suddenly looked more imposing. Was it the coat or something else? His expression looked cold and determined.

"Okay, but before we do that I need to send a quick text," smiled Jacee as if he'd finally remembered something. He slid his sleek phone out of his pocket typed something on the screen.

"What is this nonsense?" interrupted Kennedy.

Jacee didn't look up from his task. "You'll know soon enough, old man." After pressing *SEND*, Jacee replaced the mobile in his pocket and crossed his arms. "I thought maybe you'd had your chance to convince him yesterday. Well, you know me. I wanted to make sure I had my bets covered."

Jacee pointed up. Benjamin followed the celebrity's gaze and picked out three objects falling from the sky. Four seconds later, they'd settled a ways away.

Benjamin looked around Jacee to see what they were. It was three people. The boy in front looked to be in his early teens. He was attired like Jacee in stylishly faded jeans and a designer t-shirt that probably cost two hundred dollars. Even his features looked like Jacee's. The boy smiled at Trevane.

Squinting to look past him, Benjamin's gaze fell on the other two forms. His eyes widened his shock.

It was Nathan and Emily.

CHAPTER 37

ULTIMATUM

"How dare you bring…" seethed Kennedy.

"Spare me the lessons. I thought I'd bring a couple of Benjamin's closest friends to the party. I learned my lesson with that kid in Texas. This time around it's going to be a sure thing. By the way, say hello to Max," he pointed to his miniature clone. "I don't think you've met Max have you, Kennedy?"

Kennedy's face tightened. "I have not had the pleasure."

"I'll bet you're wondering how I found him before you did. Imagine that! A destructor you didn't know about. How did I do it? Let's just say that I have my ways. I won't give away my secrets. Wouldn't be much fun without them, I say."

Behind Max, Emily was crying. Nathan stood close by. His face looked like a kid trying to be brave and yet ready to run.

Jacee turned to Benjamin. "I'm sorry it came to this, Benjamin. I promise I'm not the bad guy Kennedy makes me out to be. I'm sure you'll love it when you get a taste of it. Isn't that right, Max?"

Max nodded.

"See? Max used to be nothing too. Now he travels all over the world helping me help the world. What could be better than that?"

Benjamin had finally shaken the alarm of seeing his friends. He looked up at Trevane and asked, "Why did you kidnap my friends?"

Jacee shrugged. "What can I say? Sometimes a man's gotta do what a man's gotta do. You'll learn that. Besides, they were more than happy to come along…at first."

"What are you gonna to do with them?"

"I'll come back to that question. First, let me ask, do you know where we are right now?"

Benjamin shook his head.

"This is…"

"Jacee, don't!" Kennedy yelled.

Jacee ignored his old mentor.

"I thought it only fitting that we come back to the place where it all started. Kennedy did tell you my story, right?"

"Yeah," answered Benjamin.

"Did he tell you about my parents?" A hint of bitterness laced the tone of the question.

Benjamin nodded.

Jacee swept his arm around motioning to the surrounding area.

"This is where they died."

———◆———

Fear threatened to overwhelm Benjamin. He stared at Jacee as if willing him to say it was all a big joke. It was too real. Death was something only grownups had to deal with, wasn't it?

"So you see, it's a question of life or death, Benjamin. You come with me and grow into the amazingly gifted man I know you will become, or your friends…"

The threat hung in the heat hazed air touching each of the five in different ways. Max laughed. Nathan stood in silence. Emily put her face in her hands and sobbed. Kennedy stepped closer.

"Stay where you are, old man. This is between me and Benjamin. What do you say, Benjamin?"

Benjamin looked from Jacee to Kennedy, from Kennedy to Nathan, from Nathan to Emily. He was trapped. How was ten-year-old kid supposed to make that kind of decision?

All of a sudden, three things happened. Benjamin watched it unfold like it was in slow-motion. The earth rumbled, a crash sounded and a boulder flew through the air from somewhere behind them.

Jacee's eyes gleamed with glee as he directed the flying rock at Kennedy. To his credit, Kennedy barely flinched. At the last second the boulder swerved and flew harmlessly over the old man's head, rolling until it came to a crashing halt amidst a stand of trees.

"You shouldn't have done that, son," said Kennedy calmly.

"I told you not to call me son!" screamed Jacee. All of his composure vanished. He looked like a toddler having a temper tantrum. His eyes bulged with rage and his nostrils flared. That was when all hell broke loose.

CHAPTER 38

MAYHEM

The dust was the first to rise in whirls and streams. It coiled itself around Jacee like a sandstorm. Jacee's hair stood on end propelled by the movement of the air around him.

"I'm tired of your meddling, old man," said Jacee, pointing an accusing finger at Kennedy. "It's time you saw who's really in charge."

Raising his hands and gaze skyward, Jacee laughed like a madman. Benjamin slowly backed away keeping an eye on Nathan and Emily. Kennedy hadn't moved. He looked almost bored.

Dirt and stone mixed with dead leaves and dry summer air to dull their senses. It was hard to see through the building storm. Benjamin took a last glance at Jacee, whose attention was fully focused on Kennedy, and ran toward Nathan and Emily

Max moved to stop Benjamin from reaching his friends. Jacee's protégé raised a hand like he was going to deliver a powered downward karate chop.

"Noooo!" yelled Jacee. Without shifting his stare, he pointed a finger at Max and his young clone flew back, coming to a halt twenty feet from where he'd been. "I told you not to hurt him."

Benjamin kept running.

More rocks flew. Trees uprooted and twirled through the air. Kennedy remained in his spot, ducking occasionally, calmly taking in the situation.

A visibly upset Max struggled to stand. His scraping landing had left his shirt torn and his back bleeding. He winced and shook the red dust out of his hair. With an evil grin, he turned his focus to Emily. Jacee hadn't said anything about not hurting her.

Benjamin screamed in defiance when he saw Max turn to face Emily. He pushed his legs, but it was no use. They wouldn't get him there in time.

The earth around Emily came out in one big chunk like some invisible being had stuck a huge hand into the ground and pulled Emily up with it. She was ten feet off the ground and now on her knees looking all around in horror. Max kept his concentration squarely on the young girl.

Benjamin skidded to a stop and looked up as Emily ascended atop the clump of dry red clay. His mind went back to the time he'd stopped the falling tree, the time he'd practiced in his back yard, the time he'd made himself float in the air.

Squaring his shoulders like a fighter prepping for battle, Benjamin focused his mental energy. The results were immediate. Emily's climb stopped. She and the earthen clod seemed to be vibrating in the air like some strange game of tug-a-war.

Max grunted and gritted his teeth. Benjamin felt the same strange sensation course through his body. He could almost feel Emily. In his mind's eye it was all so clear. Much as he'd done with juggling multiple items in his bedroom, a part of him shifted focus to Max. By giving a tiny mental flick, Benjamin sent the teenager flying back once again.

Nathan rushed over as Benjamin lowered Emily back down to the ground. The sound of the masked battle between Jacee and Kennedy was deafening. Crashes and cracks. Booms and thumps. They were concealed from view by the sandstorm and debris.

Emily looked up from the ground, her face covered by the fine red film of dust. Tears rolled in steady streams down and off her chin.

"Are you okay?" asked Benjamin.

"I…I think so."

"Nathan, take Emily over there," Benjamin pointed in the direction opposite the raging battle. "Find a safe place and hide until I come find you."

"But…"

"Just go. I need to help Kennedy." There was a fierce determination etched on Benjamin's dirty face. He'd turned into their leader in a matter of moments.

Emily hugged Benjamin. Nathan joined in. They stood together through the chaos not knowing if they'd ever see each other again.

Benjamin broke the embrace and looked at his friends.

"I'm sorry they brought you. I'll see you soon."

Nathan and Emily didn't know what to say. What do you say to a friend that just saved your life and might be going off to die? Instead of answering, they both nodded and ran where Benjamin had told them to go.

After checking to see that Max wasn't moving, Benjamin turned and walked into the maelstrom.

Back and forth the battle went. It was only a matter of time until one jagged rock or splintered branch would hit a combatant. Their bodies were mortal after all and someone would either get wounded or, from the sound of the fury, probably die.

Benjamin stepped into the middle of it all. It wasn't possible for him to erect a force field or shield. He'd figured that much out about his gift. That's not how it worked. Instead, like a real life video game, he had to focus on each and every thing flying in the air. Spreading his thoughts vertically, horizontally, sideway and splitways, Benjamin found he could do it without much effort. Something told him that what he was doing wasn't normal. He shouldn't be able to do it. On some level it had surprised him that he'd dispatched Max so easily. It was like he'd tapped into some limitless pit of power. His body didn't feel different. It was his mind and spirit that had changed.

Wading into the darkness of the melee, Benjamin caught a glimpse of Kennedy. A dark streak of red ran down one cheek and another had soaked his pant leg down to his ankle.

"Stop!" shouted Benjamin.

Everything did stop. Every stone, every tree, every particle floated in midair awaiting a command.

Jacee strolled around the suspended debris. He still looked spotless. It didn't look like a single piece of dirt had touched his designer jeans or manicured hands.

"My, my, Benjamin. Please tell me you took care of Max for me. Unfortunately his talent seemed to be a little…lacking. The only thing he was good at was throwing things really fast. You on the other hand…"

With a downward sweep of his hand, everything settled to the ground.

The air was now as clear as when they'd first arrived.

"Last chance, Benjamin." Jacee was casually picking at something under his fingernail. "You wanna be a loser and hang with the old crowd…or do you want to come with me and do something really special?"

"I don't want to go with you. You're…you're…"

Jacee smugness melted into simmering anger. "I'm what?"

"You only care about yourself," said Kennedy. "You say you care about other people through your charities and what not, but in reality it's all about you."

"I'm going to change the world," Jacee growled.

"I don't doubt it. But until my last breath, I promise you, I will stand in your way."

As if on cue, a sharp whistling cut through the air. Jacee smiled a split second before the tiny stone 'thrown' by Max connected with the side of Kennedy's head. The old man dropped lifelessly to the ground.

Benjamin screamed, "Nooooooo!"

CHAPTER 39

AWAKENING

Benjamin stumbled over to his mentor even as the man's life-blood spilled onto the ground. It made the boy gag, but he forced the feeling away and knelt down to try to stem the flow.

"It's what he deserved, you know," said Jacee. "He shouldn't have gotten in the way. Just leave him. There's nothing you can do."

Benjamin looked back at pop star with red rimmed eyes. "You're a murderer," spat Benjamin.

"Maybe to you. Others won't think so. Come on. Let's get you home." Jacee reached down and tried to pull Benjamin up by the arm. The young boy shook the grip off. Jacee frowned.

"Fine. Wait for him to die then we'll leave."

Max staggered over looking completely disheveled. He took up a position next to his boss.

"Nice shot, Max. I might just have to keep you around." Jacee patted his bloody clone on the back. Max grimaced from the pain. "Why don't we…"

Benjamin ignored the conversation and focused on Kennedy. He held the old man's gnarled hand as the rise and fall of his chest slowed. A single tear dropped out of Benjamin's eye and fell onto their connected hands. That's when Benjamin felt it. A warmth spread out from his core. There was no tingling. At first Benjamin thought it was a breeze blowing across the arid land. It didn't feel strange. In fact, it felt comforting and calmed his ragged breathing.

Involuntarily, he shifted his thoughts to the open wound on the side of Kennedy's head. As he watched the deep gauge first expelled blood and then seemed to swell. Benjamin's eyes widened when the wounded closed up like a zipper and Kennedy's eyes fluttered open.

"What…" murmered Kennedy.

Jacee heard the voice and rushed to look over Benjamin's shoulder. The cocky singer's face blanched.

"How…?"

Kennedy sat up slowly scratching the side of his head. He looked fine despite the dirt encrusted blood on the side of his face and his generally disheveled appearance.

Jacee and Max backed away from the scene cautiously.

Kennedy chuckled. "It looks like Benjamin's a bit more special than we believed."

Jacee was shaking his head trying to comprehend. Of course he'd heard the stories. No one ever had all the powers. The last look he gave Benjamin was one of hunger, like a panther coveting a prized kill.

"This isn't over!"

Jacee grabbed Max's arm and, a moment later, the two shot up into the hazy sky and disappeared.

"I could use a nap," said Kennedy, who was standing up to retrieve his walking stick.

"I don't understand," said Benjamin. "What happened? How did you get better?"

Kennedy looked at Benjamin, his eyes shimmering. "Don't you see, Benjamin? You're the one."

EPILOGUE

After finding Nathan and Emily, and getting a lot of hugs and gushes, the four unlikely companions whisked away on the winds of Kennedy's gift. It seemed like they'd been gone an eternity with all that had transpired.

They landed in the Dragon's backyard. No one was home so they all took turns taking showers, although Kennedy preferred to wash himself off with the garden hose. He said he'd gotten used to hose showers while working with a relief agency in Africa years before.

Benjamin found some clothes for Nathan and Emily from his parent's closet. Everything was too big, but no one cared.

Nathan kept babbling about how cool the flying had been. Apparently, all thoughts of almost dying had already faded from his mind.

Emily kept to herself and ogled at Benjamin with wonder as if seeing him for the first time. Embarrassed, Benjamin tried to ignore the looks. He didn't want things to change, but in his gut he knew they already had.

After they'd each gotten something to eat from the Dragon's well stocked fridge (Nathan ate an entire leftover extra large pizza), Kennedy sat them down at the kitchen table and told them about the gifts (there was no need to hide it now) and how important it was that they keep it a secret.

Benjamin sat stoically. Nathan bounced in his chair. Emily stared at Benjamin.

"I can't promise you that Mr. Trevane won't be back. That's why it's important that you not tell anyone about what happened. Don't worry, I'm calling in some friends that will discreetly keep an eye on you. You won't even know they're here."

"Who are they? Are they like you and Dragon?" asked Nathan.

"They are. A destructor and a healer are on their way as we speak. Don't bother looking for them. They're used to this sort of thing."

"That is so cool! I wish I could do that stuff," said Nathan.

"Does anyone have any questions?"

"Yeah. How can I get powers too?" pressed Nathan.

The stares leveled from the others in the room made him shut his mouth.

"Benjamin, I'm going to escort Nathan and Emily home. I'll be back soon."

They left Benjamin to his thoughts. He stood at the kitchen window and tousled his still wet hair that smelled like the wintergreen shower gel in his dad's bathroom. For some reason it made him want his parents. Two squirrels chased each other with feints and twists in the backyard. To them it was just another ordinary day. For Benjamin, everything was extraordinary.

Kennedy returned twenty minutes later.

"They're back safe and sound. Now, how about we have that little chat?" said Kennedy.

They walked to the backyard and sat on the stone bench that faced the overgrown grass. Something inside Benjamin bubbled and burped like a fizzy glass of soda. He was all nervous energy. Good nervous energy.

"What did you mean when you said I'm the one?" asked Benjamin, barely able to keep his happy jitters at bay. He clamped his hand on his knee and the light tapping of his foot stopped.

"Before I answer that I wanted to say thank you. Thank you for saving my life, Benjamin."

Benjamin didn't know what to say so he just nodded and turned a little pink.

"Now that that's out of the way, let's talk about my somewhat grandiose comment of you being *The One*. I suppose it's a rather loaded explanation, so I'll attempt to keep it short. As I mentioned in our very first meeting, none of our kind, at least in the past twenty or so centuries, has ever had more than one gift. We have those who develop their gifts more profoundly than others…"

"Like Jacee?"

"Yes. Like Jacee." Kennedy frowned at the thought. "As I was saying, there are differing levels of expertise within our little tribe. You, however, seem to possess more than one. Let me ask you, although I believe I know the answer, was this that first time you'd ever healed anyone?"

"Of course."

"Good. Now have you ever made anything grow, say a seed or a tree?"

"Only in science class, but everybody did that."

"Good, good. Well, I wouldn't be surprised if you experienced that soon as well."

"But…but what are you going to do about Jacee?" asked Benjamin, trying to get to the information he really wanted.

"I assume you've made the final decision *NOT* to help him?" Kennedy said, arching one bushy eyebrow like a lot of old men do.

Benjamin rolled his eyes and said, "Duuuuh."

"Very well. Then our mission is to keep you out of his hands. I'm sure you noticed how he looked at you *after* you saved my life?"

"Yeah. He looked even creepier, like the with who wanted to eat Hansel and Gretel."

"Yes, well, that's because you're now the ultimate prize. Before he knew you had the capability of being one of the most gifted. Now he knows you're one of a kind. He'll do anything he can to get his hands on you. I don't want to scare you, but you must know that we're asking you to grow up mighty quickly."

"What else is new?" shrugged Benjamin. "So what do I need to do?"

"For now, keep doing what you've been doing. Go to school, practice when you can, see if…"

Music chimed somewhere far off. It sounded like someone playing on a xylophone.

"Sorry," said Kennedy. "That's my phone."

He pulled a tiny cell phone out of his inner coat pocket and said, "Yes?"

For a minute all he did was nod. Finally he said, "I'll be there within the hour," and replaced the phone where he'd gotten it.

"Well, it looks as though Mr. Trevane has made the first move," explained Kennedy.

"What happened?"

"I'll tell you on the way." Kennedy rose from the bench, his old legs cracking as they straightened.

"I'm going with you?"

"What? Oh, of course. Would you like to try flying us there?"

"Really? But, I don't know where to go!"

"I'll show you the way. Ready to go?"

Amidst the buzzing of two bumblebees jockeying for a position on one of Mrs. Dragon's roses, Benjamin got to his feet.

Kennedy nodded and Benjamin focused on getting them into the air. It was easy now that he knew how it should feel. At first they rose slowly, Kennedy looking around to make sure no one was watching. A delighted smile made its way onto Benjamin's squeaky clean face.

"Is that as fast as you can go?" asked Kennedy adding a wink and a grin.

The smile spread to Benjamin's eyes as he looked straight up into the sky, blinked once slowly, and then sent them rocketing into the billowy heavens.

38040066R00126

Made in the USA
Middletown, DE
12 December 2016